To renew or order library books visit
www.lincolnshire.gov.uk
You will require a Personal Identification Number.
Ask any member of staff for this

F

FIELDING

The sheikh's guarded heart
(Large print)

£13.25

THE SHEIKH'S
GUARDED
HEART

THE SHEIKH'S GUARDED HEART

BY

LIZ FIELDING

MILLS & BOON®

MILLS & BOON and
MILLS & BOON with the Rose Device
are registered trademarks of the publisher.

First published in Great Britain 2006
Large Print edition 2007
Harlequin Mills & Boon Limited,
Eton House, 18-24 Paradise Road,
Richmond, Surrey TW9 1SR

© Liz Fielding 2006

ISBN-13: 978 0 263 19422 7
ISBN-10:   0 263 19422 1

Set in Times Roman 16½ on 19 pt.
16-0107-52845

Printed and bound in Great Britain
by Antony Rowe Ltd, Chippenham, Wiltshire

CHAPTER ONE

LUCY FORRESTER wasn't fooled for a minute. The insubstantial shimmer of green was a mirage.

She'd read everything she could about Ramal Hamrah, the desert. Mirages, she'd learned, were not the illusions of thirst-maddened travellers, but occurred when refracted light mirrored distant images—oil tankers, cities, trees— making them appear where they had no business to be, only for them to evaporate as the earth revolved and the angle of the sun changed.

It happened now, the momentary vision of eye-soothing green vanishing before her eyes. But even a mirage was enough to distract her from her unthinking rush to confront the man who'd betrayed her. Just because there was no traffic— no road—didn't mean that there were no hazards.

She checked the satellite navigation system, adjusted her direction slightly, then forced herself to relax her white- knuckle grip on the steering wheel a little. Look around, take her bearings.

Not that there was much to see apart from the mountains—clearer, sharper now that she was on higher ground away from the coast. There was nothing green here, only the occasional scrubby, dust-covered bush in an otherwise dry and empty landscape.

Her eyes, seared and aching from a sun that mocked her delicately tinted sunglasses, felt as if they were filled with sand and she would have welcomed another glimpse of the cooling green. Even an illusion would do.

Dehydrated, hungry, she should have realized that she'd need more than rage to sustain her, but her bottle of water had long been empty. And, shaken to bits by her charge across the corrugated surface of the open desert, her entire body felt as if it had been beaten black and blue.

She didn't understand it. According to the map, it was no more than a hundred and fifty miles to Steve's campsite. Three hours, four at the most. She should have been there long before now.

She closed her eyes momentarily, in an attempt to relieve them. It was a mistake. Without warning the 4x4 tipped forward, throwing her against the seat-belt as the ground fell sharply away in front of her, wrenching the wheel from her hands. Before she could react, regain control, the front offside wheel hit something hard, riding up so that the vehicle slewed sideways, tipped drunkenly, and after a seemingly endless moment when it might, just, have fallen back four-square on the ground, the rear wheel clipped the same unseen rock and the world tipped upside down.

Only the bruising jolt of the seat-belt against her breastbone, shoulder, hip, stopped her from being tumbled around the interior like washing in a drier as the vehicle began to roll.

It didn't stop her arms from flailing uncontrollably, bouncing against the wheel, the roof, the gear stick. Didn't stop her legs from being pounded against the angles of a vehicle built for function, rather than comfort. Didn't stop everything loose from flying around, battering her head and neck.

It seemed an eternity before the world finally stopped turning and everything came to a halt.

For a while that was enough.

When, finally, she managed to focus on her surroundings, the world was at an odd angle, but the silence, the lack of any kind of movement, was deeply restful and Lucy, glad enough to rest quietly in the safety cage of her seat-belt, felt no urgent need to move.

At least the green was back, she thought. Closer now. She tried to make sense of it through the crazing of the safety glass.

Trees of some kind, she decided, after a while. It was the fact that they were upside down that had confused her. That they were below, rather than above a high wall.

Had she stumbled across the Hanging Gardens of Babylon?

No, that couldn't be right. Babylon wasn't in Ramal Hamrah. It was… Somewhere else.

Maybe she was dead, she thought dispassionately.

Heaven would be green. And quiet. Although the gate she could see set into the wall was not of the pearly variety promised in the fire-and-brimstone sermons preached at the church her grandmother had attended, but were carved from wood.

But then wood was, no doubt, more precious than pearls in a place where few trees grew.

Wall and door were both the same dull ochre as the desert. Covered with centuries of wind-blown dust, they were all but invisible unless you were looking directly at them or, as now, intense shadows cast by the lowering sun were throwing the carvings into relief.

The angel looked real enough, though, as he flew down to her on wings of gold.

Gradually tiny sounds began to impinge on her consciousness. The ticking of the engine as it cooled. Papers fluttering. It was her diary, she saw, lying amongst the jumble of stuff thrown from her bag, the pages riffling in the wind, blowing her life away. She closed her eyes.

Moments, or maybe it was hours, later she opened them to a pounding beat that sounded oddly familiar but which she couldn't quite place. And the slow drip, drip, drip of something leaking.

Coolant or brake fluid, she thought.

She ought to do something about that. Find the hole, plug it somehow or she'd really be in trouble…

Stirred from her dazed torpor, she began to tug feebly at the seat belt but was brought to an instant halt by a searing pain in her scalp. Confused, in pain as a hundred smarts, bruises and worse were jolted into life, she kept still, tried to focus her energy, find the strength to reach the release catch, free herself, without tearing her hair out by the roots.

Then the smell of petrol reached her.

Petrol dripping on to hot metal…

It was a wake-up call to the danger she was in; forget heaven, she was at the gates of hell and raw, naked fear overrode pain as she struggled to twist herself around to hit the seat belt release.

Her sweaty fingers slipped as she tried to make contact and, as the smell of petrol grew stronger, she panicked, throwing herself against the restraints—

'Hold still, I've got you.'

She heard the words, but they didn't penetrate the thinking part of her brain as she fought to break free.

'Don't move!'

It wasn't the harsh order that shocked her into motionless silence, or the fierce, hawk-like features of the man who gave it. It was the gleaming knife blade, so close to her face that she could almost taste the metal at the back of her throat.

It was one shock too many.

Hanif al-Khatib cursed as the woman fainted dead away, then braced himself to catch her as he cut her free from the seat belt, trusting to luck as to whether he did more damage as he hauled her dead weight up through the open window of the 4x4 and on to his saddle. The smell of petrol filled the hot air and there was no time to waste doing the thing gently as, holding her limp body tight against him with one arm, he urged his horse to safety.

When the vehicle burst into flames he was still close enough to feel a flare of heat that made the desert air seem momentarily icy.

Time passed in a blur of pain. Lucy heard voices but could not understand what they said. The only comfort was in the dusty cloth beneath her face, the steady beat of a human heart, soft re-assuring words. Someone was holding her close, not letting go. With the part of her brain that was still functioning, she knew that as long as he held her she would be safe.

Nothing short of an emergency would have induced Hanif al-Khatib to set foot in a hospital. He hated everything about them—the smell, the hushed careful voices of the staff, the high-tech sound of machines measuring out lives in bleeps rather than heartbeats. Announcing death in a high-pitched whine that drilled through the brain.

The overwhelming sense of guilt…

His aide had done his best to keep him away from the emergency room, to persuade him to remain in the desert, assuring him that he could manage.

He didn't doubt it; Zahir was more than capable, but he came anyway, needing to assure himself that everything necessary was done for the woman. And because a lone foreign woman driving across the desert as if the hounds of hell were after her had left him with the uneasy suspicion that there was more to it than a simple accident.

Since he hadn't delayed to change his clothes

and they, and the *keffiyeh* wound about his face, bore the dust of a day's hunting, no one had realised who he was and that suited him well enough. The last thing he wanted was to attract the attention of local media; he valued his own privacy and the young woman he'd rescued was unlikely to welcome the attention, speculation, that being brought into casualty by the son of the Emir was likely to arouse.

He'd left all direct contact with the hospital staff to Zahir, staying in background, content to be thought nothing more than muscle brought along to carry the woman pulled from the wreck of her vehicle.

Nevertheless, the arrival at the hospital of a helicopter bearing the Emiri insignia would have raised more than passing interest and he was eager to be away. Just as soon as he satisfied himself that the woman was not seriously injured, would be properly cared for.

He turned from the window as Zahir joined him in the visitors' room. 'How is she?'

'Lucky. They've done a scan but the head injuries are no more than surface bruising. At worst, mild concussion.'

'That's it?' He'd feared much worse. 'She was fainting, incoherent with pain in the helicopter,' he pressed.

'She's torn a ligament in her ankle, that's a world of pain, and she took quite a battering when the vehicle rolled.'

'That's lucky?'

Zahir pulled a face. 'But for you, Excellency, it would have been a lot worse.'

'I was simply the nearest. The first to reach her.'

'No one else would have risked riding straight down the *jebel* as you did.'

The boy did not add that no one else had had so little regard for his own safety, although he was clearly thinking it. Not true. With a broken neck he would have been no use to her.

'The woman owes you her life.'

He dismissed the idea with an impatient gesture. 'Is she being kept in the hospital?'

'That won't be necessary,' Zahir said. 'She just needs to rest for a few days.' Then, 'I've informed the pilot that we're ready to leave.'

Hanif had done his duty and now that he knew the woman would make a full recovery there was nothing to keep him. Except that she had looked so fragile as she'd struggled to free herself.

'You've spoken to someone at Bouheira Tours?' he asked, pushing the image away. 'They have contacted her family? Someone is making arrangements to look after her, get her home?'

Zahir cleared his throat. 'You need not concern yourself, Excellency,' he said. Then, forgetting himself in his anxiety to leave, 'We need to go, Han, already rumours are flying around the hospital—'

He didn't ask what kind of rumours. A foreign woman had been brought to the hospital in a helicopter used by the son of the Emir. What they didn't know, they'd make up.

'Put a stop to them, Zahir. The girl was found by a hunting party, my staff offered humanitarian aid. I was not involved.'

'I'll do what I can.'

'So?' he persisted. 'Who is she? Does she work for this company? Or is she just another sand-surfer, tearing up the desert as if it's her personal playground?'

He hoped so. If he could write her off as some shallow thrill-seeker, he could forget about her.

'The tourist industry is becoming an important part of our economy, Excellency—'

'And, if so, why was she travelling alone, in the wrong direction to anywhere?' Hanif continued, ignoring Zahir's attempt to divert his attention.

Too inexperienced, too young to hide what he was thinking, his young cousin hesitated a moment too long as he decided just how much to tell him. Just how much he dared leave out.

Hanif moved to the nearest chair, turned, sat down with a flourish that no one could have mistaken for anything but regal and, with a gesture so slight as to be almost imperceptible, so imperious that not even a favoured cousin would dare ignore it, invited the boy to make up his mind.

'Sir—' Zahir swallowed, saw there was no help for it and finally admitted the truth. 'Bouheira Tours say they have no idea who this woman might be. She does not work for them and they were adamant that she could not be a client. They have no women in any of the parties booked this week.'

'Yet she was driving one of their vehicles.' He

waited. 'Their logo was emblazoned on its side. Desert safaris, dune-surfing,' he prompted.

'I made that point.'

'Who did you speak to?'

'The office manager. A woman called Sanderson. The man who actually owns the company, Steve Mason, is in the east of the country, guiding a party of archaeologists who have come to look at the ancient irrigation systems.'

'She was heading too far north to have been joining them.'

'She may have been lost.'

'Surely their vehicles are fitted with satellite navigation equipment?' Zahir made no comment. 'So, what explanation did this Sanderson woman have for the fact that a woman she'd didn't know was driving one of their vehicles?'

'She didn't. She said we must be mistaken. That none of their vehicles is missing. She pointed out that there are other companies running desert trips. That, since the vehicle was burned out, we may have been mistaken.'

'You were there, Zahir. Do you believe we were mistaken?'

Zahir swallowed. 'No, sir.'

'No. So, when you assure me that our casualty is to be looked after, what exactly did you mean? That the hospital will contact her embassy where some official will draw up a document requiring her to repay them the cost of medical treatment and repatriation before they'll do a damn thing to help her?'

'I assumed you would wish to have her treatment to be charged to your office, sir. Other than that—'

'Always assuming that she can prove her identity,' Hanif continued as if he hadn't spoken. 'Her nationality. It might take some time, since everything she was carrying with her was incinerated. Who will care for her in the meantime?'

'You saved her life, Han. You have done everything required.'

'On the contrary, Zahir. Having saved her, I am now responsible for her.' A situation he would have otherwise, but to wish that he hadn't become involved would be to wish her dead and that he could not do. 'Who is she?' he demanded, as keen as anyone to see an end to this. 'What's her name?'

'She gave her name as Lucy Forrester.'

'Did she say where she was going?'

'No. It was because she seemed so confused that they ordered a scan.'

'And the doctor says she can be discharged?' Then, on his feet and at the door before Zahir could open his mouth, he said, 'Never mind. I'll speak to him myself.'

'Sir!'

Hanif strode down the corridor, ignoring the boy's anguished plea.

'Excellency, it is my duty to insist—'

As he turned on him the boy flinched, stuttered to a halt. But he bravely stood his ground.

'You've done everything that is required,' he repeated. 'There can be no doubt that she's British. Her embassy will take care of the rest.'

'I will be the judge of when I have done everything required, Zahir.' Then, irritably, 'Where is he? The doctor?'

'He was called to another emergency. I'll have him paged for you.'

'No.' It wasn't the doctor who held him where he least wanted to be, but his patient. 'Where is *she*?'

There was another, almost imperceptible, pause before, apparently accepting the inevitable, Zahir said, 'She's in the treatment room. The last door on the left.'

Lucy Forrester was looking worse, rather than better than when he'd carried her into the A and E department.

In his head, he was still seeing her in that moment before she'd fainted, with long hair spread about her shoulders, fair skin, huge grey eyes. Since then the bruising had developed like a picture in a developing tank; her arms were a mess of ugly bruises, grazes, small cuts held together with paper sutures and there was dried blood, like rust, in her hair.

The hospital had treated her injuries—her right leg was encased below the knee in a lightweight plastic support—but the emergency team hadn't had time to do more than the minimum, cleaning up her wounds, but nothing else. Presumably that was the job of the ward staff.

For now, she was lying propped up, her skin clinging to fine bones, waiting for someone to decide where she was going. She looked, he thought, exhausted.

Her eyes, in that split second before she'd lost consciousness, had been wide with terror. Her first reaction now, starting, as if waking from a bad dream, was still fear and, without thinking, he reached for her hand. Held it.

'It's all right, Lucy,' he said. 'You're safe.'

Fear was replaced by uncertainty, then some other, more complex, emotion that seemed to find an echo deep within him.

'You saved me,' she mumbled, the words scarcely distinguishable through her bruised, puffy lips.

'No, no,' he said. 'Lie back. Take your time.'

'I thought… I thought…'

It was all too clear what Lucy Forrester had thought, but he did not blame her. She'd been hysterical and there had been no time for explanations, only action.

He released her hand, bowed slightly, a courtesy that would not normally be afforded to any woman other than his mother, his grandmother, and said, 'I am Hanif al-Khatib. You have friends in Ramal Hamrah?' he asked. Why would a woman travel here alone except to be with someone? 'Someone I can call?'

'I—' She hesitated, as if unsure what to say. She settled on, 'No. No one.' Not the truth, he thought. Not the whole truth, anyway. It did not matter.

'Then my home is at your disposal until you are strong enough to continue your journey.'

One of her eyes was too swollen to keep open. The other suggested doubt. 'But why—?'

'A traveller in distress will always find help, refuge in my country,' he said, cutting off her objection. He was not entirely sure 'why' himself, beyond the fact that he had not rescued her from death to abandon her to the uncertain mercy of her embassy. At least with him, she would be comfortable. And safe. Turning to Zahir, he said, 'It is settled. Make it happen.'

'But, Excellency—'

Hanif silenced him with a look.

'Go and find something warm for Miss Forrester to travel in. And send a nurse to clean her up. How could they leave her like this?'

'It may be a while,' his cousin said, disapproval practically vibrating from him. 'They're rushed off their feet in A and E.'

Lucy watched as her Samaritan impatiently waved the other man away before turning to the cupboards where dressings were stored, searching, with growing irritation until he finally emerged with a stainless steel dish and a pack of cotton wool. He ran water into the bowl, tearing off chunks of cotton and tossing them in to soak.

'I'm not a nurse,' he said, turning to her, 'but I will do my best to make you more comfortable.'

'No,' she said, scrambling back up against the raised headboard. 'Really, there's no need.'

'There is every need,' he said. 'It will take Zahir a little while to organise the paperwork.' He didn't smile, but he was gentleness itself as he took one her hands, looking up in concern as she trembled. 'Does that hurt?'

'No,' she managed.

He nodded, as if that was all he needed to know, and began to gently wipe the damp cotton pads over her fingers, her hands, discarding the pads as each one became dirty.

And it was, after all, just her hands.

It was nothing, she told herself. She wouldn't object to a male nurse doing this and the man had saved her life. But his touch, as he carefully wiped each finger as if they were made of something fragile and fine, did something unsettling to her insides and a tiny sound escaped her. Not nothing…

He glanced up enquiringly and she managed to mouth, 'It's okay.'

Apparently reassured, he carefully washed away the dirt and dried blood from the bruised back of her hand before turning it over to clean the palm. He moved to her wrist, washed every bit of her arm with the same care.

Then he began again on the other hand. Time was, apparently, of no importance.

He emptied the bowl, refilled it. 'Fresh water for your face,' he said, and she swallowed. Hands, arms were one thing. Her face was so much more personal. He'd have to get closer. 'I… Yes…'

'That's too hot?' he enquired, as she jumped at the touch of a fresh pad to her cheek, let out an incoherent squeak.

'No…' The word seemed stuck in her throat but she swallowed it down and said, 'No, it's just…' It was just that her grandmother's brainwashing had gone deep. Bad girls let men touch them. In her head she knew that it wasn't like that, that when people loved one another it was different, but even with Steve she'd found the slightest intimacy a challenge. Not that he'd pressed her.

He'd assured her that he found her innocence charming. That it made him feel like the first man in the world.

Innocent was right. No one but an innocent booby would have fallen for that line.

While she knew that this was different, that it had nothing to do with what her grandmother had been talking about, it didn't make it any easier, but she managed a convincing, 'It's fine…' refusing to let fall tears of rage, remorse, helplessness—a whole range of emotions piling up faster than she could think of words to describe them. After a long moment in which the man waited, apparently unconvinced, she said, 'Truly.'

'You must tell me if I hurt you,' he said, gently lifting the hair back from her face.

All she wanted was for him to get on with it, get it over with, but as he gently stroked the cotton over her skin it was just as it had been with her hands, her arms. He was tenderness itself and her hot, dry skin, dehydrated and thirsty, seemed to soak up the moisture like a sponge.

'I'm just going to clean up your scalp here,' he warned. 'I think you must have caught your hair when you were struggling with the seat belt.' It stung a little. Maybe more than a little because he stopped, looked at her and said, 'Shall I stop?'

'No. Really. You're not hurting me.' Not much anyway.

Pride must abide.

Words chiselled on to her scalp.

He lifted her long tangled hair, holding it aside so that he could wash the nape of her neck, and she gave an involuntary sigh. If she could only wash her hair, she thought, she'd feel a hundred times better.

'Later,' he said. 'I will wash your hair tomorrow.'

She was smiling into the soft wool *keffiyeh* coiled around his neck before she realized that he'd answered her unspoken thoughts. She considered asking him how he'd done that. Then waited. If he was a mind-reader she wouldn't need to ask…

There was a tap on the door and someone called out.

He rapped out one word. He'd spoken in Arabic but the word was unmistakable. *Wait.* Then he laid her back against the headrest and she whispered, '*Shukran.*' Thank you.

She'd bought a teach yourself Arabic course, planning to learn some of the language before joining Steve. She hadn't just want to be a silent partner. She'd wanted to be useful. A bit of a joke, that. She'd served her usefulness the minute she'd so trustingly signed the papers he'd placed in front of her.

Hanif al-Khatib smiled at her—it was the first time, she thought. The man was so serious... Then he said, '*Afwan,* Lucy.'

Welcome. It meant *welcome,* she thought. And she knew he meant it.

In all her life, no one had ever treated her with such care, such consideration, as this stranger and quite suddenly she was finding it very hard to hold back the dam of tears.

Obviously it was shock. Exhaustion. Reaction to the accident...

She sniffed, swallowed. She did not cry. Pain,

betrayal, none of those had moved her to tears. She'd learned early that tears were pointless. But kindness had broken down the barriers and, embarrassed, she blinked them back.

'You are in pain, Lucy?'

'No.'

He touched a tear that lay on her cheek. 'There is no need to suffer.'

'No. They gave me an injection. I just feel sleepy.'

'Then sleep. It will make the journey easier for you.' Then, 'I will return in a moment,' he said.

She nodded, her mind drifting away on a cloud of sedative. She jerked awake when he returned.

'I hope you will not mind wearing this,' Hanif said, helping her to sit up, wrapping something soft and warm around her, feeding her arms into the sleeves.

She had no objection to anything this man did, she thought, but didn't have the energy to say the words out loud.

'How is she?'

Hanif had left Zahir in Rumaillah to make en-quiries about his guest and now he roused himself to join him in the sitting room of the guest suite.

'Miss Forrester is still sleeping.'

'It's the best thing.'

'Perhaps.' She'd been fighting it—disturbed, dreaming perhaps, crying out in her sleep. It was only the sedatives prescribed by the hospital keeping her under, he suspected. 'What did you discover in Rumaillah? Was the embassy helpful?'

'I thought it better to make my own enquiries, find out what I could about her movements before I went to the embassy. If you want my opinion, there's something not quite right about all this.'

'Which is, no doubt, why you tried to dissuade me from bringing her here,' Hanif replied, without inviting it.

'It is my duty—'

'It is your duty to keep me from brooding, Zahir. To drag me out on hunting expeditions. Tell my father when I'm ready to resume public life.'

'He worries about you.'

'Which is why I allow you to stay. Now, tell me about Lucy Forrester.'

'She arrived yesterday morning on the early flight from London. The immigration officer on duty remembered her vividly. Her hair attracted a good deal of notice.'

He didn't doubt it. Pale as cream, hanging to her waist, any man would notice it.

Realising that Zahir was waiting, he said, 'Yes, yes! Get on with it!'

'Her entry form gave her address in England so I checked the telephone number and put through a call.'

'Did I ask you to do that?'

'No, sir, but I thought—'

He dismissed Zahir's thoughts with an irritated gesture. 'And?' he demanded.

'There was no reply.' He waited for a moment, but when Hanif made no comment he continued. 'She gave her address in Ramal Hamrah as the Gedimah Hotel but, although she had made a booking, she never checked in.'

'Did someone pick her up from the airport, or did she take a taxi?'

'I'm waiting for the airport security people to come back to me on that one.'

'And what about the vehicle she was driving? Have you had a chance to look at it? Salvage anything that might be useful?'

'No, sir. I sent out a tow truck from Rumaillah, but when it arrived at the scene, the 4x4 had gone.'

'Gone?'

'It wasn't there.'

'It can't have vanished into thin air, Zahir.'

'No, sir.'

Hanif frowned. 'No one else knew about it, other than the woman at Bouheira Tours. What did you tell her?'

'Only that one of their vehicles had been in an accident and was burnt out in the desert. She was clearly shaken, asked me to describe it, the exact location. Once I had done that she said that I must be mistaken. That the vehicle could not belong to them. Then I asked her if Miss Forrester was a staff member or a traveller booked with them and she replied that she'd never heard of her.'

'She didn't want to check her records?'

'She was quite adamant.'

'Did you tell her that Miss Forrester had been injured?'

'She didn't ask what had happened to her and I didn't volunteer any information.'

'Leave it that way. Meanwhile, find out more about this tour company and the people who run it. And Zahir, be discreet.'

CHAPTER TWO

THE room was cool, quiet, the light filtering softly through rich coloured glass—lapis blue and emerald, with tiny pieces of jewel-bright red that gave Lucy the impression of lying in some undersea grotto. A grotto in which the bed was soft and enfolding.

A dream, then.

Lucy drifted away, back into the dark, and the next time she woke the light was brighter but the colours were still there and, although she found it difficult to open her eyes more than a crack, she could see that it was streaming through an intricately pieced stained glass window, throwing spangles of colour over the white sheets.

It was beautiful but strange and, uneasy, she tried to sit up, look around.

If the tiny explosions of pain from every part

of her body were not sufficiently convincing, the hand at her shoulder, a low voice that was becoming a familiar backdrop to these moments of consciousness, assured her that she was awake.

'Be still, Lucy Forrester. You're safe.'

Safe? What had happened? Where was she? Lucy struggled to look up at the tall figure leaning over her. A surgical collar restricted her movement and one eye still refused to open more than a crack, but she did not need two good eyes to know who he was.

Knife in his hand, he'd told her to be still before. She swallowed. Her throat, mouth were as dry as dust.

'You remember?' he asked. 'The accident?'

'I remember you,' she said. Even without the *keffiyeh* wound about his face she knew the dark fierce eyes, chiselled cheekbones, the hawkish, autocratic nose that had figured so vividly in her dreams.

Now she could see that his hair was long, thick, tied back at the nape with a dark cord, that only his voice was soft, although the savage she'd glimpsed before she'd passed out appeared to be under control.

But she knew, with every part of her that was female, vulnerable, that the man who'd washed her as she lay bloody and dusty on a hospital couch was far more dangerous.

'You are Hanif al-Khatib,' she said. 'You saved my life and took me from the hospital.'

'Good. You remember.'

Not that good, she thought. A touch of amnesia would have been very welcome right now.

'You are feeling rested?'

'You don't want to know how I'm feeling. Where am I?'

Her voice was cracked, dry, and he poured water into a glass then, supporting her up with his arm, held the glass to lips that appeared to have grown to twice their size. Some water made it into her mouth as she gulped at it. The rest dribbled down her chin, inside the collar.

He tugged on the bow holding it in place and removed it, then dried her face, her neck, with a soft hand towel.

'Should you have done that?' she asked nervously, reaching for her throat.

'Speaking from experience, I can tell you that the collar doesn't do much good, but the doctor advised keeping it in place until you were fully awake.'

'Experience? You crash cars that often?'

'Not cars. Horses.' He gave a little shrug. 'Perhaps it would be more accurate to say that they crashed me. Polo makes great demands on both horse and rider.'

'At least the rider has the choice.' Then, 'Where am I? Who are you?' His name and 'safe' told her nothing.

'When I lived in England,' he said, 'my friends called me Han.'

'When I lived in England...'

Her brain felt as if it was stuffed with cotton wool, but she was alert enough to understand that this was his way of reassuring her that he understood western expectations of behaviour. Why would he do that unless she had reason to be nervous?

'What do your enemies call you?' she snapped back, pain, anxiety, making her sharp. She regretted the words before they were out of her mouth; whatever else he was, this man had saved her from a terrible death. But it was too late to call them back.

His face, his voice expressionless, he replied, 'I am Hanif bin Jamal bin Khatib al-Khatib. And my enemies, if they are wise, remember that.'

Her already dry mouth became drier and she shook her head, as if to distance herself from what she'd said. Gave an involuntarily squeak of pain.

'The doctor prescribed painkillers if you need them,' he said distantly.

'No,' she said. 'Thank you.' She was finding it hard enough to think clearly as it was and she needed all her wits about her. Needed answers. 'You told me your name before,' she said. Only this time there was more of it. Steve had explained about the long strings of names and she knew that if she could decipher it she would know his history. '*Bin* means "son of"?'

He bowed slightly.

'You are Hanif, son of Jamal, son of…'

'Khatib.'

'Son of Khatib, of the house of Khatib.' The name sounded familiar. Had Steve mentioned it? 'And this is your home?'

Stupid question. Not even the finest private room in the fanciest hospital had ever looked like this. The carved screens, folded back from the window, the flowered frieze, each petal made from polished semi-precious stone, furniture of a richness that would have looked more at home in a palace…

'You are my guest, Miss Forrester. You will be more comfortable here than in the hospital. Unless you have friends in Ramal Hamrah with whom you would rather stay? Someone I could contact for you?' he continued. 'We tried calling your home in England—'

'You did?'

'Unfortunately, there was no reply. You are welcome to call yourself.' He indicated a telephone on the night table.

'No.' Then, because that had been too abrupt, 'There's no one there.' No one anywhere. 'I live alone now. I'm sorry to be so much trouble,' she said, subsiding into the pillows, but not before she'd seen the state of her arms. The cuts had been stuck together, the grazes cleaned, but the effect was not pretty.

'Don't distress yourself. They'll heal very quickly. A week or two and they'll be fine.' Then, 'Are you hungry?'

'I don't want to put you to any more trouble,' she said. 'If I could just get dressed, impose on you to call me a taxi.'

'A taxi?' He frowned. 'Why would you need a taxi?'

'To take me to the airport.'

'I really would not advise it. You should take a day or two to recover—'

'I can't stay here.'

'—and it will undoubtedly take that long to replace your passport, your ticket. I'm sorry to have to tell you that everything that you were carrying with you was destroyed in the crash.'

'Destroyed?' Without warning she caught a whiff of petrol amongst the mingled scents of sweat, dust, disinfectant that clung to her. 'They were burned?' And she shivered despite her best effort not to think about how close she had come to being part of the conflagration. 'I need to see someone about that,' she said, sitting up too quickly and nearly passing out as everything spun around her.

'Please, leave it to my aide. He will handle everything,' he assured her. 'They will be ready, *insha'Allah,* by the time you're fit to travel.'

'Why are you doing this?' she demanded. 'Why are you being so kind to me?'

He seemed surprised. 'You are a stranger. You need help. I was chosen.'

Chosen?

She put the oddity of the expression down to the difference in cultures and let it go, contenting herself with, 'You pulled me out from the car wreck. For most people that would have been enough.' Then, realising how ungrateful that must have sounded, 'I know that I owe you my life.'

That provoked another bow. '*Mash'Allah*. It is in safe hands.'

For heaven's sake! Enough with the bowing…

'I'm in no one's hands but my own,' she snapped back.

She might owe him her life, but she'd learned the hard way not to rely on anyone. Not even those she'd had a right to be able to trust. As for the rest…

'We are all in God's hands,' he replied, without taking offence, no doubt making allowances for her injuries, shock, the fact that sedatives tended to remove the inhibitions. Her grandmother hadn't held back when she'd finally surrendered to the need for pain relief. A lifetime of resentment and anger had found voice in those last weeks…

'I'm sorry,' she said carefully. 'You're being extremely kind. I must seem less than grateful.'

'No one is at their best when they've been through the kind of experience you've endured,' he said gravely.

This masterly, if unintentional, understatement earned him a wry smile. At least it was a smile on the inside; how it came out through the swellings and bruises was anyone's guess.

'You need to eat, build up your strength.'

She began to shake her head and he moved swiftly to stop her. 'It would be better if you did not do that,' he cautioned, his hand resting lightly against her cheek. 'At least for a day or two.'

She jumped at his unexpected touch and he immediately removed his hand.

'What can I offer you?'

What she wanted most of all was more water, but not if it meant spilling half of it down herself like a drooling idiot.

Maybe she'd said her thoughts out loud, or maybe he'd seen the need in her eyes as she'd looked at the glass, because he picked it up, then sat on the edge of the bed, offering his arm as a prop, but not actually touching her. Leaving the decision to her.

'I can manage,' she assured him, using her elbows to try and push herself up. One of them buckled beneath her and all over her body a shocking kaleidoscope of pain jangled her nerves. Before she fell back he had his shoulder, his chest, behind her, his arm about her in support, taking all her weight so that her aching muscles didn't have to work to keep her upright.

'Take your time,' he said, holding the glass to her lips. Raising her hand to steady it, she concentrated on the glass, avoiding eye contact, unused to such closeness, such intimacy. He did not rush her, but showed infinite patience as, taking careful sips this time, she slaked what seemed to be an insatiable thirst. 'Enough?' he asked when she finally pulled back.

She nearly nodded but remembered in time and instead glanced up. For a moment their gazes connected, locked, and Lucy had the uncomfortable feeling that Hanif bin Jamal bin Khatib al-Khatib could see to the bottom of her soul.

Not a pretty sight.

Hanif held the glass to Lucy's lips for a moment longer, then, easing her back on to the pillow, turned away, stood up. Her body had seemed feather-light, as insubstantial as gossamer, yet the weight of it had jarred loose memories that he'd buried deep. Memories of holding another woman in just that way.

Memories of her dark eyes begging him to let her go.

From the moment he'd cut Lucy Forrester free of the wreck she'd been attacking his senses, ripping away the layers of scar tissue he'd built up as a wall between himself and memory.

She smelt of dust, the hospital, but beneath it all her body had a soft, warm female scent of its own. He'd blocked it out while he'd held her safe on his horse, cradled her as she'd whimpered with pain, drifting in and out of consciousness in the helicopter, other, more urgent concerns taking precedent. But now, emergency over, he could no longer ignore the way it filled his head. Familiar, yet different.

He could not tell if it was the familiar or the different that bothered him more. It did not matter, but he clung to the glass as if it was the only thing anchoring him to earth as he took a deep steadying breath.

He was no stranger to the sick room, but this was more difficult than he'd imagined. Dredging up the poignant, painful memories he'd worked so hard to obliterate from his mind.

She is different.

And it was true. Noor had been dark-eyed, golden-skinned, sweet as honey. The unsuspected, unbreakable core of steel that had taken her from him had lain well hidden within that tender wrapping.

Lucy Forrester was nothing like her.

The difference in their colouring was the least of it. His wife had been strong, steady, a rock in a disintegrating world, but this woman was edgy, defensive, troubled, and he sensed that she needed him in a way that Noor never had.

The glass rattled on the table as he turned back to her. 'I'm sure you would enjoy some tea,' he said. 'Something light to eat?'

'Actually, right now, all I want is the bathroom. A shower. To wash my hair.'

Lucy Forrester shuffled herself slowly up

against the pillows, obviously finding it painful
to put weight on her bruised elbows, but determined to have her way.

He knew how she felt. He'd taken hard falls
back in the youthful, carefree days when he'd
thought himself indestructible. Had chafed impatiently through weeks laid up with a broken leg.

'That's a little ambitious for your first outing,'
he suggested. 'Maybe if I brought a bowl of
water, you could—'

'I'm not an invalid. I've just got a few bumps
and bruises,' she said, then let out an involuntary cry as she jerked her shoulder.

'That hurt?' he enquired, with an edge to his
voice he barely recognised, annoyed with her for
being so obstinate.

'No,' she snapped. 'I always whimper when I
move.' Then, 'Look, I know you're just trying to
help, but if you'll point me in the direction of the
bathroom I can manage. Or did you want to come
along and finish what you started in the hospital?'

'I apologise that there are no women in my
household to help you. If you think you can
manage—'

'Too right, I can. I'll bet you wouldn't allow

your wife to be washed by some strange man, would you? Probably not even a male nurse.'

There were men he knew, members of his family even, who would not allow their wives to be examined by a male doctor, let alone be touched by a male nurse. He had long since passed that kind of foolishness.

'I would willingly have let my wife be cared for by a Martian if I'd thought it would have helped her,' he said.

Would have? Past tense?

Oh, no, Lucy thought, she wasn't going there…

'Look, I know you're just trying to help and I'm grateful, but I'll be fine once I'm on my feet.'

He looked doubtful.

'Honestly! Besides, it's not just a wash I need and I'm telling you now, you can forget any ideas you might have about trying out your bedpan technique on me.'

'You are a headstrong woman, Lucy Forrester,' he said. 'If you fall, hurt yourself, you may end up back in the hospital.'

'If that happens, you have my full permission to say I told you so.'

'Very well.' He glanced around as if looking for something, and said, 'One moment.' And with that he swept from the room, dark robes flowing, the total autocrat.

Oh, right. As if she was planning to hang around so that he could enjoy the spectacle of her backside hanging out of the hospital gown.

Sending encouraging little you-can-do-it messages to her limbs, she pushed the sheet down as far as she could reach. Actually it wasn't that far and, taking a moment to catch her breath, she had to admit that she might have been a bit hasty.

Ironic. All her life she'd been biting her tongue, keeping the peace, not doing anything to cause a fuss, but the minute she was left to her own devices she'd done what her grandmother had always warned her about and turned into her mother.

Impulsive, impetuous and in trouble…

If Hanif bin al-thingy hadn't been passing she'd have been toast, she knew, and it wasn't worth dying over.

Money.

She'd been broke all her life and when she'd had money she hadn't known what to do with it.

At least Steve had given her a few weeks of believing herself to be desired, loved.

He might be a cheat, a liar, a con man, but he'd given value for money. Unfortunately there were some things that she couldn't just chalk up to experience and brush aside. Which was why she had to get out of here...

Everything was going fine until she swung her legs over the edge of the bed and tried to stand up. That was when she discovered what pain really was.

She didn't cry out as she crumpled up on the floor. She tried, but every bit of breath had been sucked out of her and she couldn't make a sound, not even when Hanif dropped whatever he was carrying with a clatter and gathered her up, murmuring soft words that she didn't understand; the meaning came through his voice, the tenderness with which he held her.

Idiot! Han could not believe he'd been so stupid. He was so used to total obedience, to having his orders obeyed without question, without explanation, it had never occurred to him that Lucy would ignore his command to stay put until he found the crutches, the ankle splint, which had been tidied away by someone as he'd dozed on the day bed in the sitting room.

Over and over he murmured his apologies and only when she let her head fall against his shoulder and he felt her relax, did he gently chide her.

'You could not wait two minutes, Lucy?'

'I thought I could manage. What have I done?' she asked into his shoulder. 'What's wrong with me?'

'You've torn a ligament in your ankle, that's all.'

'All?' She looked up.

'I know,' he sympathised. 'It is an extremely painful injury.'

She remembered.

At the time it had all happened so quickly that she'd felt nothing. It had been just one pain amongst many. Now, though, she was reliving the moment in slow motion…

He was holding her, supporting her, holding the sheet to her mouth before she even knew she was going to need it, but there was nothing to throw up except water…

By the time her stomach caught up with reality

and gave up, she was sweaty and trembling with weakness. He continued to hold her, offering her water, wiping her forehead, her mouth—so gently that she knew her lips must look as bad as they felt.

'You're very good at this,' she said, angry with him, although she couldn't have said why. Angry with herself for having made such a mess of everything. 'Are you sure you're not a nurse?'

'Quite sure, but I took care of my wife when she was dying.'

His voice, his face, were wiped of all emotion. She wasn't fooled by that.

She'd become pretty good at hiding her feelings over the years, at least until Steve had walked into her life; he'd certainly cured her of that. But when you knew how it was done it was easy to spot.

'I'm so sorry…Han,' she said, trying out the name he'd offered, as near as she could get to an apology for behaving so badly, so thoughtlessly, when all he was doing was trying to help her. When he was clearly reliving all kinds of painful memories.

'Nausea is to be expected,' he said distantly.

That wasn't what she'd been apologising for

and she was sure he knew it. Questions crowded into her mind, but she had no right to ask him any of them and she let it go. Better to keep to the practicalities.

'Didn't they explain your injuries to you at the hospital?'

'They tried. I didn't understand most of what they were saying. I was just so confused. By everything.' She looked up, appealing for understanding. 'I saw a mirage,' she said, trying to make him see. 'At least I thought I did. Then, after the crash there was an angel. He had gold wings and he was coming to get me and I thought I was dead—'

'Hush, don't distress yourself—'

'And then you were there and I thought... I thought...'

She couldn't say what she'd thought.

'You drifted in and out of consciousness for a while. The mind plays tricks. The memory becomes uncertain.'

'You're speaking from experience again?' she asked, trying a wry smile, but suspecting that it lost something of its subtlety in translation from her brain to her face.

'I'm afraid so.' Then, 'They did a scan at the hospital,' he said, wanting to reassure her. 'There was no head injury.'

'Just my ankle? Really? Is that it?' she asked. 'No more nasty surprises?'

'Lacerations and bruising.'

'Cracked ribs?'

'No one mentioned anything about cracked ribs,' he said, finally showing some emotion, if irritation counted as emotion, although not, she thought, with her. 'Are they sore?'

'Everything is sore. So, tell me, what's the prognosis?'

'The bruises, abrasions, will heal quickly enough and you'll need to wear a support on your ankle for a couple of weeks, use crutches. That's where I went. To fetch them for you.'

'Oh. I didn't know.'

'Of course you didn't. I should have explained.' His smile was a little creaky, as if it needed oiling, she thought. 'I'm so used to being obeyed without question.'

'Really? I hate to have to tell you this, Han, but western women don't do that any more.'

'No? Do you want to take a shower?'

'Please…'

'Then you're going to have to do as you are told.'

'What…?' Catching on, she laughed and said, 'Yes, sir!'

'Hold on,' he said and she didn't hesitate, but grabbed at his shoulders, bunching the heavy dark cloth of the robe he was wearing beneath her fingers as he lifted her back up on to the bed.

Her laughter caught at him, tore at him, and he did not know which was harder, taking her into his arms or letting her go so that he could fasten the support to her ankle. He reached out to stop her tipping forward when she was overcome by dizziness.

'I'm fine,' she assured him. 'Just pass me the crutches and give me some room.'

He didn't try to argue with her, but he didn't take any notice of her either, Lucy discovered. The minute she had the crutches in her hands, had settled them on the floor ready to push herself up, she found herself being lifted to her feet.

She would have complained, but it seemed such a waste of breath.

He didn't let go either, but just leaned back a

little, spreading his hands across her back to support the shift in weight. Strong hands. Hands made to keep a woman safe.

He was, she thought, everything that Steve was not.

A rock, where the man she'd married in such haste was quicksand.

Light-headed, drowning in eyes as black as night, her limbs boneless, she knew that if she fell into Hanif al-Khatib's arms the world would turn full circle before she needed to breathe again.

'Lucy…'

It was a question. She thought it was a question, although she wasn't sure what he was asking.

She swallowed, shocked at the thoughts, feelings, that were racing through her body—struggled to break eye contact, ground herself.

'I'm all right.' Breathless, her words little more than a murmur, he was not convinced. 'You can let go.' Then, when he still didn't move, 'I won't fall.'

She looked down and slowly, carefully, felt for the floor beneath her one good leg, took her weight. Then she leaned on the crutches. Still he held her, forcing her to look up.

'Please,' she said.

Han could not let go. It was as if history was repeating itself, that if he stopped concentrating, even for a moment, she would fall, be lost to him.

Stupid.

She was nothing to him.

He was a man without feelings.

Yet from the moment her dust trail had caught his eye his world had become a torrent of emotions. Irritation, anger, concern...

He refused to acknowledge anything deeper.

'We'll do it my way,' he said abruptly, taking a small step back, without removing his support. 'Or not at all.'

'It's that instant obedience thing again, isn't it?' she said.

'Try it. You might like it.'

She blew a strand of hair from her face, took the weight on her hands and swung forward a few inches, barely stopped herself from crying out in pain. For a moment his entire body was a prop for hers, her forehead against his cheek, her breast crushed against the hardness of his broad chest, her thighs, clad in nothing but a skimpy hospital gown, against the smooth, heavy cloth of his dark robes. And, as he held her, for one giddy moment she felt no pain.

'This is harder than it looks,' she admitted after a moment.

'You are not ready,' he said, tucking the loose strand of hair behind her ear, doing his best to ignore the silky feel of it.

'Thanks,' she said. 'I usually wear it tied back. I really must get it cut the minute I get home.'

'Why?' he asked, horrified. 'It's beautiful.'

'It's a damned nuisance. I meant to do it before…'

'Before?'

She shrugged. 'Before I came to Ramal Hamrah. Okay, I'm ready. You can let go now.'

Against his better judgement, he took another step back, still keeping a firm hold of her.

In this manner, her persistence wearing down his resistance, they crossed the room one step at a time until they were standing in the bathroom with the wall at his back. 'This is as far as we go.' Then, when she was slow to respond, 'Enough, Lucy,' he said impatiently. 'You've made it to the shower. You can drop the crutches. I have you. You won't fall.'

Lucy's leg was shaking from the effort, her hands, arms, shoulders, back, shrieking in agony. It wasn't that she wouldn't obey Han, it was because she couldn't. Her fingers were welded to the crutches and she was unable to straighten them.

'I can't,' she said.

Looking down, he saw her problem and, muttering something she did not understand, but was sure was not complimentary, he caught her around the waist and, propping her up against his body, eased the crutches from her grasp.

'You've done enough for today,' he said.

Lucy, the hot grittiness of her skin made all the more unbearable by the very nearness of relief, persisted. 'I'm not leaving here until I've had a shower.'

He shook his head, smiling despite himself. 'I have to give you ten out of ten for determination, Lucy Forrester.'

'Yes, well, no one ever accused me of being a quitter. And look, the shower has a seat. Easy. Just turn it on, give me back the crutches and leave me to it.'

He did as she'd said, testing the water until he was certain it was not too hot or cold, making sure that she had everything she needed to hand before turning to go. 'Do not,' he said, 'lock the door.'

'Got it,' she said—as if she had the energy to waste on that kind of nonsense. Then, clutching hold of a handrail, 'If I need you I'll scream. Deal?'

'Deal.'

'Oh, wait. Um, can you unfasten the bows at the back of this thing?'

Keeping his gaze fixed firmly above her head, he tugged the fastenings loose on her hospital gown. 'Anything else?'

'No. Thank you. I can manage.'

It was an exaggeration, but she did what she had to, then settled herself in the shower, keeping her splinted foot propped out of the way of the water as much as she could. The warm water seemed to bring her back to life, but washing her hair was more than she could manage and by the time she'd struggled into the towelling robe he'd laid out for her she was almost done.

'Han?'

He was there almost before the word was out of her mouth.

'Thanks,' she said, swinging herself through

on willpower alone. 'I would have opened it myself, but I had my hands full.'

'You, Lucy Forrester, *are* a handful,' he said. 'Come, there is food, tea. Eat, then you can rest.'

Hanif had hoped for a few minutes alone walking the quiet paths of the ancient garden surrounding the pavilion where Lucy Forrester lay resting.

Fed by a precious natural spring that irrigated the orchards, guarded from the encroaching desert and wandering animals by thick, high walls, they had been laid out centuries earlier as an earthly reflection of heaven and he'd come here hoping to find some measure of peace.

In three years he hadn't found it but today it wasn't his own guilt and selfishness that disturbed him. He'd barely reached the reflecting pool before an agitated Zahir came hunting him down.

'Sir!'

Han stopped, drew a deep breath then turned, lifting his head as the tops of the trees stirred on a windless day. Knowing what Zahir was going to say before the words left his mouth.

'Sir, I've had a signal from the Emir's office.'

No one had been here in months so this was no coincidence; it had to be something to do with Lucy Forrester.

'Who is it?' he asked. 'Who is coming?'

Was it the man—he was certain it would be a man—she'd been so desperate to reach?

'It is the Princess Ameerah, sir.'

Not her lover, then, but nevertheless Lucy Forrester was the direct cause of this invasion.

'I am to have a chaperon, it would seem. You wasted no time in reporting last night's event to my father, Zahir.'

'Sir,' he protested. 'I did not. I would not…' Then, 'Your father is concerned for you. He understands your grief but he needs you, Han.'

'He has two other sons, Zahir. One to succeed him, one to hunt with him.'

'But you, Han…'

'He can spare me.'

Zahir stiffened. 'You were not recognised at the hospital, I would swear to it, but the removal of Miss Forrester by your staff would not have passed without comment. Sir,' he added, after a pause just long enough to indicate that he did not appreciate his loyalty being doubted. 'It was only a matter of time before news of it reached your father.'

'He will want to know why the news did not come from you.'

'You undertook a simple act of charity, Excellency. I did not believe the incident was of sufficient importance to interest His Highness.'

'Let us hope, for your sake, that His Highness takes the same view,' Hanif replied wryly, briefly touching the young man's shoulder in a gesture that they both understood was an apology. 'I would hate to see him replace you with someone less concerned about bothering him.'

Or was that what Zahir was banking on? Did he consider the chance of returning to the centre of things worth the risk of irritating the Emir?

'I think I should warn you, Zahir, that the arrival of the princess would suggest otherwise.'

'It may be a coincidence.'

'I don't believe in coincidence.' Undoubtedly his father was making the point that if he could take in and care for some unknown foreign woman, he could spare time for his own daughter. He turned away. 'Make the necessary arrangements to receive the princess.'

'It has been done, Excellency.' Zahir raised his voice as the helicopter appeared overhead, shaking a storm of blossom from the trees. 'Will you come and greet her?'

'Not now. She'll be tired from her journey. Maybe tomorrow,' he said when his cousin looked as if he might press the point.

He'd had three years of tomorrows. One more wouldn't make any difference.

CHAPTER THREE

LUCY had refused the painkillers Han offered, but he'd left the two capsules beside the bed with a glass of water in case she changed her mind, and a small hand bell that she was to ring if she needed anything, before leaving her to rest.

She was, she had to admit, feeling exhausted, but it wasn't just the effects of the accident. She hadn't slept since the second credit card statement had arrived. The first she'd assumed was a mistake, had emailed Steve and he'd said he'd sort it out. When the second one had arrived a couple of days later she'd known that the mistake was all hers.

Her body jabbed her with irritable reminders of what she'd put it through with every movement, but for the moment she'd chosen what passed for clear-headedness over relief.

She needed to think, try and work out what to do. How much to tell Hanif al-Khatib. She didn't want him to get into trouble, but neither did she relish the thought of being turned over to the authorities, which was what he would have to do once he knew the truth.

Her research on the Internet at the library had informed her that Ramal Hamrah was a modern state that paid due respect to human rights; what that meant in terms of punishment for car theft, justifiable or otherwise, she had no idea. And actually she was finding it hard to convince herself that her actions were justifiable.

Gran wouldn't have thought so, but then she'd taken an unshakeable Old Testament line when it came to sin. Thou shalt not…

The only certainty in her own life these days was that she'd behaved liked an idiot. If she'd gone to the police, instead of taking off after Steve like some avenging harpy, she wouldn't be in this mess. Now she'd lost the moral high ground, had put herself in the wrong.

Maybe a good lawyer could get her off on the grounds that the balance of her mind had been disturbed, she thought. Hold him responsible for everything. Make a counter-claim against him, at least for the fraud.

But what good would that do? Even if she could afford a lawyer, Steve wouldn't be able to repay her if he was in jail.

Besides, it was no longer just about the money.

That was what was so unfair. When she'd taken the 4x4 and set off to look for him it hadn't been herself she'd been thinking of. All she'd wanted was for him to put things right…

As if.

That was the point at which she decided that a clear head was not so very desirable after all but, as she reached for the painkillers, she re-alised that she was not alone.

'Hello.' Lucy forced her swollen face into a smile. The tiny girl, exotic in bright silks, half hiding behind the open door, didn't move, didn't speak, and she tried again, using her limited Arabic. '*Shes-mak?*' What's your name? At least she hoped that was what it meant since the child's only response was a little gasp of fright before she took off, tiny gold bangles tinkling as she ran away.

Her place in the doorway was immediately

taken by a breathless figure, a lightweight black *abbeyah* thrown over her dress, who paused only long enough to gasp her own quickly muffled shock before murmuring, 'Sorry, sorry…' before disappearing as fast as her charge.

Did she look that bad?

There must have been a mirror in the bathroom—there was always a mirror above the basin, even in her grandmother's house where vanity had been considered a sin.

Maybe some inner sense of self-preservation had kept her from examining the damage but now she wondered just how grotesque she looked. Was she going to be permanently scarred?

She raised her hands to her face, searching for serious damage. Everything was swollen—her lips, her eyes, the flesh around her nose. None of her features felt…right, familiar.

Han had moved the crutches, the plastic splint, had propped them up out of the way on the far side of the room. It didn't matter, she had to know the worst. Putting her sound foot down, she heaved herself upright, grabbing the night table for support.

For a moment every muscle, every sinew,

every bone, complained and it was touch and go whether the table would fall or she would.

She didn't have a hand to spare to catch the painkillers as they spilled on to the floor, or the glass which followed them, toppling over, spilling water as it spun before falling on to the beautiful silk carpet. Then the bell succumbed to gravity, landing with a discordant clang, followed by the crash of the telephone.

There was nothing she could do about any of it; all she could do was hold on tight and pray.

Apparently that was enough.

After a moment the room stopped going round and, since she wasn't sure what would happen if she put her weight on her damaged ankle, she used her good one to hop across the room, hanging on to the table, the wall, the door, jarring every bone in her body, but gritting her teeth, refusing to give up.

Once she reached the door, however, she was on her own. It seemed an unbridgeable distance to the basin, but she wasn't about to give up now and, with desperate lurch, she reached her goal.

It was only when she finally recovered her breath sufficiently to turn and confront her reflection, that she realised all her effort had been for nothing.

There had once been a mirror over the basin—the fittings were there—but it had been removed.

Did she look that bad?

Without warning her legs buckled beneath her and, still hanging on to the basin, she crumpled up in a heap on the floor. For a moment she sat there in shock. Then, as she tried to move, haul herself back up, she discovered that she hadn't got the strength to do it, which left her with two choices.

She could shout for help or crawl back to bed on her hands and knees.

She was still trying to get herself up on to her knees when Han folded himself up beside her.

'Can I not leave you for a moment, Lucy Forrester?'

She shrugged, forced a smile—or more probably a grimace.

'I guess I'm not cut out for total obedience.' She forced a smile—or more likely a grimace—and said, 'I was doing okay until I was overcome by gravity.'

'Don't knock gravity. Without it we'd be in

serious trouble.' Then, 'I thought we'd agreed that you would ring the bell if you needed anything.'

'Did we?' As a slave to her grandmother's bell, she was somewhat averse to them. 'You said I should; I don't recall agreeing to it. Besides, I thought you'd try to stop me.'

'Why would I do that?'

'I wanted to look at my face. I scared a little girl. She ran away when I spoke to her. I needed to know the worst.'

'Ameerah? She was here?'

'Is that her name? She looked really frightened, the poor child.'

'Poor child, nothing,' he said dismissively. 'She ran away because she was caught where she shouldn't have been.' He got up and offered her his hands. 'Come along, let me get you back to bed.'

It was a clear change of subject and, although she was curious, Lucy thought it wiser to leave it at that. But she made no move to accept his support.

'I still want to see the damage,' she said. 'If I look so bad that you took the mirror away—'

'No!' He seemed at a loss, she thought. 'No,

it was nothing to do with you. The mirror was broken. A long time ago. You look…' Words failed him.

'That bad?'

He shook his head. 'You have some bruising, that's all. It looks worse than it is.'

'How much worse? Do I have a black eye?'

He hesitated. 'Not exactly.'

'Not exactly black?'

'Not exactly one,' he admitted with a wry smile. 'And really, they're more an interesting shade of purple. With yellow highlights.'

'An overrated colour scheme, I've always thought,' she replied, equally wry, but omitting the smile. 'Anything else?'

'There are a few minor cuts, nothing that will leave a scar. And your bottom lip is swollen.' He looked as if he was going to say more, but thought better of it.

'And?'

He gave the kind of shrug that suggested she'd be wiser to leave it at that.

'And?'

'It would seem that there was a bag loose in the car. It must have caught your cheek…' he touched a finger to her cheekbone '…here,' he said, lightly tracing a curve first one way, then the other.

'My Chanel bag?' she said, realising that it had gone up in flames with everything else.

Han glanced up, looked into her eyes. Then, suddenly distant, 'I'm sorry you lost it. I hope it was insured.'

'I hadn't got around to it,' she admitted. 'Don't worry, it was almost certainly a fake.'

'You don't know?'

'It was a gift.'

He frowned as if he didn't understand. Clearly he would never have given anyone a knock-off as a gift. Would certainly never have pretended it was the real thing.

'Maybe I'm being unkind,' she said, although in the light of recent events it seemed unlikely that Steve would have paid for the genuine article.

He didn't pursue it. 'I hope you're reassured that there's no permanent damage to your face, Lucy, but in any case I'll have the mirror replaced for you.'

'No rush,' she said, finally placing her hands in his, allowing him to help her to her feet, to put his arm around her waist and support her back to bed. 'Now you've given me a blow by blow description, I'm in no great hurry to see the reality for myself.'

Someone, she noticed, had picked up the pills she'd dropped. The water and broken glass had been cleaned up too, the bell and telephone were back in place.

'Han…' She had to tell him about the 4x4. He had to know that he was harbouring a criminal. A wanted woman. 'There's something I have to tell you—'

'Take the painkillers the doctor gave you, Lucy,' he said, cutting her short as he lowered her on to the bed. For a moment she sat there, his arm still around her, his cheek close enough to feel the warmth emanating from his skin. Then, abruptly, he moved, lifted her legs, turning her so that she could lie back in comfort. Covered her with the sheet. 'You need to rest, give your body a chance to recover. There is nothing you have to say that will not wait until tomorrow.'

Maybe he was right. He'd want to know why she had stolen the four-wheel drive, what she had been doing out in the desert on her own. To tell him would mean betraying Steve, with consequences beyond her control. She needed to think it through properly.

He'd picked up the capsules and offered them to her and, after a moment, she took them, swallowed them.

'If you need anything, please, just ring the bell. Someone is always near.'

Whatever was in the capsules had to be more than simple painkillers because within minutes she was sinking fast into sleep but, before she went under, her mind snagged on the one question she hadn't asked.

Who was the little girl?

And why had he said that there were no women in his house?

She might even have cried the words out loud as she was dragged under by the sedative because, far away, she was certain that he answered her.

Han watched Lucy slide into unconsciousness; she was troubled, tried to speak even as sleep claimed her, but trouble, as he knew, did not go away. Whatever was on her mind would wait

until morning and he murmured some meaningless soothing words.

Apparently satisfied, she finally let go, slept
and, dismissing the *faraish* who had been on
duty in the adjoining sitting room ready to find
him at a moment's notice should Lucy need him,
he opened the doors to the balcony and sat
watching as night drew in and the stars began
their journey across the night sky. Breathing in
air heavy with scent of jasmine.

A thin crescent moon rose and set. The
darkness faded to grey, then lilac. He was finally
roused, cold and stiff, when Lucy Forrester
called from the inner room.

'Hello… Is there anyone there?'

'Is the bell not working?' he asked, opening
the door from the balcony into her room.

She scowled at it. 'Ringing a bell for attention
is a bit princessy, don't you think?'

'You have no desire to be a princess?'

'I'll bet Cinderella had trouble making the
leap,' she said. 'From ringee to ringer.'

'Quite possibly.' It had been his intention to
tease her a little for her reticence. Living in the
company of men, his horses, hawks, for so long,

he'd clearly lost his touch. 'How do you feel?' he asked, deciding that it was safer to stick to the basics.

'Better, thank you.' Then, glancing to the window where the soft light that preceded dawn was filtering through the shutters, throwing bars of coloured light across the room, 'I thought I'd been asleep for longer.'

'You've slept the clock round, Lucy. That's not sunset, it's dawn.'

Her long sleep had done its work, he thought. It would take days for the swelling to go down, longer for the bruising to fade, but she looked much brighter and seemed to be moving more easily too. And the colour in her face was not entirely the result of her accident.

'Would you like to join me for breakfast?' he asked. 'Outside on the balcony.'

The invitation came from nowhere; the private meals he'd shared there with Noor, with time running out for both of them, had been precious moments, hoarded in his memory. Breakfast had long since lost it charm, ceased to be a meal to linger over; it was a long time since food had been anything but a necessity. But once voiced, however much regretted, the invitation could not be withdrawn.

Besides, the cool morning air would be good for Lucy and over breakfast she would have a chance to unburden herself.

'I'll bring your crutches,' he said, without waiting for an answer.

'Right.' Despite the half-closed eye, a split lip, she somehow managed a smile. 'This comes under the heading of total obedience, does it?'

He should return her smile, reassure her, put her at her ease. He'd learned the art at his father's knee. As a diplomat he'd practised it in the highest circles. When was the last time he'd done it for real? Not simply a going-through-the-motions movement of facial muscles, a polite response, but really smiled?

He had, he found, no difficulty in pinpointing the exact day. The exact moment.

He didn't try the diplomatic variety on Lucy Forrester. She deserved better.

'On the contrary, Lucy. I am at your command.' He picked up the telephone receiver and pressed a button. 'Tell me what you would like to eat.' Then, when she hesitated, 'Please, just say.'

'Orange juice?'

She was so uncertain. How could such a woman lack the confidence to ask, demand what she wanted, needed?

'Orange juice,' he agreed. 'And tea? Coffee?'

'Tea. Thank you.'

'And to eat?'

'Anything. Really.'

At that point he gave up prompting her and ordered a selection of food for her to choose from.

'It will be a few minutes,' he said when it was done and, picking up the robe that he had found for her, holding it so that she could slip her arms into the sleeves, said, 'plenty of time for you to practice your new found skills.'

After her shower Han had produced a full length cream silk nightgown, the kind donned by glamorous film stars way back in the days when they'd worn more than a spray of scent to bed, and a matching robe. Not new, for which he'd apologised, but clearly something that had belonged to his wife.

She wrapped the robe about her, moved, under

her own steam, to the bathroom and finally joined him outside on a broad balcony. Shaded by an ornate wooden roof, trailed by scented jasmine, it ran the entire length of the building.

Below them was a formal garden divided by long rills of water that opened up at regular intervals into pools, clustered with lilies. There were almond trees in blossom, twining around slender cypresses stretching into a wilder distance. It seemed to go on for ever. When she lifted her eyes to the horizon all she could see beyond the trees were dark mountains, peaks already turning golden as the sun rose behind them.

'How beautiful!' she said as he held a chair back for her, relieved her of the crutches. 'What is this place?'

'In ancient times the Persians called it a *pairidaeza,*' he said.

'It sounds like paradise,' she said. 'Actually it looks like paradise.'

'In modern Persian they use the same word for both paradise and garden, but a *pairidaeza* is simply a place with a wall around it. This is known as Rawdah al-'Arusah,' he said, pouring a glass of orange juice, handing it to her as she repeated the words, glanced at Hanif for a translation. 'The Garden of the Bride.'

'Oh...'

For one terrible moment she thought the bride was his, but even before he shook his head she realised her mistake. This was old. Centuries old. 'The original pavilion—' he indicated the building they occupied '—this garden, was built by one of my ancestors for his Persian bride, homesick for the garden she'd left behind.'

'All this for one woman? He must have loved her a great deal.'

'That surprises you?'

'Yes. No...' Confused, and not a little embarrassed, she said, 'I imagined that marriages among the wealthy would have been arranged. Alliances between great families. Just as they once were in England.'

'Of course. It is expected that suitable marriages will be arranged, to strengthen ties between allies, to unite those who were once enemies.'

She did not miss the present tense and said, 'It is still your custom?'

'Matters of such importance cannot be left to chance.'

She sipped the juice. Made no comment.

'You think it cold? Passionless?'

'You've just described a business transaction,' she pointed out.

'When a man and a woman come to an alliance with honour, the knowledge that their future has been written for the benefit of family and state, love and duty are one,' he replied.

Love and duty.

Her life, until a few weeks ago, had been entirely a matter of duty. There had been precious little love in it.

Then, in an instant, everything had changed.

She put down the glass, flexing the fingers of her left hand which had, until yesterday—was it only yesterday?…no, the day before that—worn a plain gold band. Unused to wearing a ring of any kind, it had felt odd, uncomfortable, on her finger, yet now it was gone she missed its reassurance. That heady, unaccustomed status of being a woman who the world could see was loved.

Realising that he was watching her, a slight

frown creasing his forehead, she asked, 'Is it that easy?'

'Nothing of worth is easy. All partnerships require effort, understanding, compromise, if they are to work.'

'You discount initial attraction? Did you meet your wife before your betrothal?'

'Not before the contract was signed.'

'And yet you loved her.'

'You doubt that happiness can be achieved between two people united in such a manner?'

'Actually, when you put it like that I can see that I would have been much better served by such a clearly understood arrangement.'

'You were married?' He sounded surprised and she remembered how carefully he'd washed each of her fingers; presumably he'd noted the absence of a wedding ring. Which was undoubtedly why he'd used the past tense.

'I am married,' she said with reluctance. 'I was married six weeks ago.'

'Six weeks?'

This time he was not simply surprised, he was openly astounded.

'Your husband can bear to let you out of his

sight so soon?' He spoke as a man whose culture could not conceive of such a thing. With derision for a man who took so little care of that which was his. Or possibly for a woman could not keep her man close.

Whichever it was, his attitude was entirely alien and yet she would have welcomed a little of his honour, his notion of love bound to duty in her own ill-fated union.

If she'd been offered an old-fashioned alliance, a contract that laid out the terms in black and white, giving her the security of marriage, the glamour of being the wife of a man like Steve Mason in return for the inheritance that she had never expected anyway, she might still have thought herself luckier than she had any right to expect.

Instead Steve had tricked her, cheated her, taken everything and given nothing, which was why she'd thrown the ring that he'd put on her finger, that had chafed at her skin, into a Ramal Hamrah gutter.

Now, clinging to all that was left to her—pride—she lifted her head and said, 'My husband had urgent business to attend to.' That was what he'd told her; it was probably the only thing he had said that was the truth.

'So urgent that you have decided not to bother him with your accident?'

Belatedly, it occurred to Lucy how this must look to Han. That she was taking advantage of his generosity when she had a husband whose duty it was to care for her. Who might, for all he knew, take violent exception to the fact that another man had usurped his place, touched his wife, held her so intimately.

Or had she, as the wife of another man, somehow compromised him?

'I'm so sorry, I should have told you straight away. My presence must be a dreadful embarrassment to you. I'll leave—'

He reached out, catching her hand as she turned, reaching for the crutches.

'No,' she said. 'Really, you can see how much better I am—'

'On the contrary, Lucy Forrester,' he cut in, 'you need time to recover your strength. You are welcome to stay in my house for as long as you need sanctuary.'

'Sanctuary?' she repeated, staring at his hand,

wrapped around hers. Strong, sinewy, without a trace of softness, yet he held her as gently as he would an injured bird.

'I have used the wrong word?' he asked. 'It means a place of refuge, does it not?'

'Well, yes. It's just…' She forced herself to look up, meet his gaze. 'Sanctuary is a word more usually used to describe a place of safety for someone on the run from danger, in fear of their life, even. Of asylum,' she added, when he made no comment.

'We are all running from something, Lucy, even if the demons at our heels are nothing but shadows.' Then, as if suddenly aware that he'd overstepped some invisible boundary, he let her go, picked up a dish—a diversion, she thought, to give them both time to recover.

'In my case they're not exactly shadows,' she said, still feeling the cool strength of his fingers against her skin. This was not a man to deceive. He deserved nothing less than the truth. 'You have a right to know that the vehicle I was driving, that I wrecked, did not belong to me.'

He paused in the act of spooning yoghurt into

a dish, regarding her steadily. 'It was rented?' he enquired. 'Borrowed?'

A tiny prickle along her spine warned her that he already knew what she was going to say.

'Not rented. Not borrowed. Steve told me he owned Bouheira Tours, but he may have lied about that. He lied about everything else. If he did, then I stole it.'

He handed her the dish of yoghurt and said, 'This is very good. It is made from milk produced by our own goats. Can I offer you honey, fruit, to flavour it?'

She ignored his gesture towards a dish of fresh fruit. 'Didn't you understand what I said?'

'You took the 4x4 from Bouheira Tours without permission.'

'A fine distinction, but not one that would impress the courts, I imagine.'

'Possibly not.' He served himself yoghurt, took some dates from the dish, bit into one. 'I recognised their logo, of course, and naturally they were the first people we contacted. We assumed you were an employee or a client of theirs. That they would take care of you.'

'Then you knew all along. I should have

realised. What did they say? Am I going to be charged with theft?' Her heart was beating like a drum. Was that why he'd bought her here, to keep her from running away?

'It may interest you to know that Bouheira Tours not only denied knowledge of anyone by the name of Lucy Forrester, but they were adamant that none of their vehicles is missing.'

'But I...' She sat back, frowned. 'But I took it from their yard. The keys were in it and I thought...' He waited, but she couldn't begin to explain exactly what she'd been thinking. 'You saw it, Han. You must have done. Their name was plastered all over it.'

'A clerical error, no doubt,' he said. 'But if they insist they aren't missing a vehicle, they can hardly make a fuss about its disappearance. And even if they belatedly realise their mistake, be assured that your shadows cannot penetrate my walls.'

Walls?

She glanced at the mountains, so close in the clear morning light. They had been nothing more than a shimmer through the heat haze when she'd landed at the airport.

'We are out in the desert, aren't we? This is where I crashed?' She turned to Han. 'I saw high walls…glimpsed green just before the accident. I told you, I thought it was a mirage.' She considered what that meant. What he'd said about a *pairidaeza,* the sheer scale of it. 'All this…' without taking her eyes off him she swept her arm in a wide gesture to take in the vastness of the gardens '…all this is behind walls? In the middle of nowhere?'

'The walls are necessary to protect the spring that waters the garden, to keep out wandering animals who would graze the garden back to desert in the blink of an eye.' Then, 'You would prefer to be in Rumaillah? The city.'

'No!' she said without thinking. 'No…'

'It can be arranged. My house there is closed up, but my mother or my sisters would, I'm sure, be happy to take you in.'

If he asked them. The fact that he hadn't asked suggested they wouldn't be exactly thrilled at the prospect. Which made his own concern for a stranger all the more worthy. Especially one who had committed a criminal act.

'No, really,' she assured him. 'I'll be fit in a day

or two and once I have my tickets, a passport, I'll be out of your hair. No need to bother anyone else.'

'Take as long as you need to regain your strength before you confront whatever troubles you.'

'Why do you insist that I am troubled?'

'No one who is at peace steals a vehicle, or risks her life as you did.'

She had no answer to that.

'Eat,' he said. 'Try the figs; they have been picked especially for you.'

He picked up a purple fruit with a bloom on its skin, handed it to her. Then took another and bit into it. Obviously, the subject of the stolen vehicle, any discussion of her departure, had been dismissed and to pursue either seemed rude. Instead she looked at the heavy fruit filling her palm, so different from the dried figs that had been a feature of her grandmother's Christmas sideboard. She'd hated those chewy, pippy things, but this was nothing like them and, somewhat cautiously, she bit into it, uncertain quite what to expect.

As the fresh sweetness filled her mouth she gasped in surprise, catching the juice that trickled down her chin with her hand, staring at the red flesh with astonishment.

'That's amazing! So different!'

He laughed too, apparently delighted with her delight. Then, as if caught unawares by the sound and horrified by it, he got up and strode away from her, putting the length of the balcony between them, before gripping the ornate wood rail as if it was the only thing stopping him from throwing himself to the stone path twenty feet below.

He looked so alone that Lucy felt an almost overwhelming urge to follow him, wrap her arms around him and pull his head down on to her shoulder in a simple gesture of comfort. Reassure him that it was all right to go on living. That laughter was not a betrayal.

It was probably a good thing that crutches made any such gesture out of the question.

She didn't know what he was going through, how he was suffering. She knew nothing of comfort, love, tenderness, and, having barely lived herself, she was in no position to offer advice to anyone else on how it should be done.

Unable to do anything useful and certain that

he would rather she ignored his loss of control and left him to gather himself, she instead forced herself to give her complete attention to the breakfast that had been provided for her.

There were a great many covered dishes and lifting the lids she discovered scrambled eggs, goat's cheese, olives, tomatoes, slices of cold meat that she thought must be lamb.

Her pathetic inability to just say what she wanted, she realised, had meant extra work for Han's staff and a shocking waste of food.

She did what she could to make amends.

Keeping her eyes politely averted from the dark, motionless figure of her host, whose gaze seemed riveted to the far mountains, she took a little of the yoghurt, laced it with honey.

Han, she discovered, was difficult to ignore and, unable to help herself, she glanced up. He had not moved, yet the still, warm air seemed to vibrate with his presence and she saw at that moment how a woman could have looked at him for the first time and fallen in love with him.

Every line of his body was charged with power, strength, grace.

His eyes were fierce, his profile carved from

granite, yet she was certain that when he had taken Noor's hand, held her for the first time, he would have been tender.

She could not have helped but love him.

Her throat tightened and her eyes stung. Would Steve have been tender too? If he hadn't been called away to some emergency, would he have made her feel like a queen? Her reward for being so gullible, so naïve?

She too found it necessary to spend a moment or two contemplating the peace of the garden before forcing herself to eat a spoonful of scrambled egg with a little thin crisp toast.

She was struggling to lift a heavy silver teapot when Han said, 'Leave it, I will do that.'

Her hand trembled slightly as he took it from her, held her fingers for a moment as if to reassure her that she would regain her strength quickly, before pouring tea into two cups.

'I apologise for abandoning you. I have black moments when memory overwhelms me and I am not fit company for man or beast,' he said, placing a cup before her.

She had no comprehension of such grief, but resisted the urge to offer spurious platitudes. Yet to say nothing, ignore his pain, change the subject to something bland and safe was not an option.

'How long is it, since you lost her?'

For a moment she thought he would not answer, but then he said, 'Three years. It has been three years since Noor died.'

He sank back into a high cane armchair and closed his eyes, whether to discourage her curiosity or to block out the memory she couldn't say, and it took courage to press on. 'Noor? I've heard the name before.'

'It was chosen by the American wife of the late King of Jordan.'

'Maybe that's what I was thinking of.'

'Maybe.' He opened his eyes, turned to look at her. 'Once we were married she was known as Umm Jamal. The mother of Jamal.'

Lucy knew that the best thing for him was to talk, that as a neutral listener, someone to whom he could tell anything, safe in the knowledge that she would be gone within days, she was the ideal person. But as if it was not difficult enough that this was an unfamiliar culture and the possibilities for insult were endless, Han seemed to be locked within a minefield of pain; her only way forward was to prompt his confidence with the questions that came to her and pray that they would not explode in her face. She owed him that much.

'The name of your son was chosen even before you were married?' she asked.

'I am the son of Jamal.' With a barest gesture with one of those long hands, he suggested that was explanation enough. Then, because obviously for her it was not, 'I will be the father of Jamal, *in sha'Allah.* It is our way.'

'I see.'

She sipped her tea.

'My wife died from leukaemia,' he said, after a seemingly endless silence in which she sought a way to phrase the impossible question.

'Leukaemia? But surely... I thought...' The words escaped her before she stopped them.

'You thought that this is a disease from which most people recover.'

There was something about the way he finished the sentence for her that made her wary about leaping in. An edge to his voice.

'You're right, Lucy; with prompt treatment most people do recover, but Noor was pregnant when she was diagnosed. She refused to accept the treatment that would have saved her in case it hurt the baby she was carrying.'

Lucy's hand flew to her mouth to block an anguished cry, but no sound could have made it through the painful lump in her throat.

To have cherished an unknown, unseen son or daughter so much; to have made the conscious decision to put her precious baby's life before her own…

How pitiful her own problems seemed in comparison.

'I told her that there would be other babies,' he said, his voice distant, as if he was not talking to her, but to someone unseen. 'That even if there weren't it did not matter. That she would always be Umm Jamal.' He turned to her, his face an expressionless mask, nothing but skin over bones. 'Nothing would move her. She would not save herself. Not even for me.'

'And Jamal?' she asked. A son given at such cost must surely be the most cherished gift. Had the sacrifice been in vain?

'Her child was born, healthy and strong,' he assured her.

Her child?

And then she knew. There had not been a son, but a daughter. The little girl she'd frightened with her bruised and swollen face.

'Ameerah.' He did not deny it. 'She must give you such solace.'

A frown creased his wide brow, as if he did not understand. 'Solace?'

'She is Noor's gift to you. A part of herself. A precious daughter.'

'She knew. All the time she was telling me that she was sacrificing herself for Jamal, she knew the baby she was carrying was a girl.'

'She was a mother protecting her unborn child,' she said. Surely he must see that?

'She lied to me!'

She flinched at the ferociousness of his response, let out an involuntary cry as all the aches that had settled to a low background hum were jerked back into life by the spasm.

'Lucy, I'm so sorry…' He reached out as if to comfort her.

'I'm fine,' she snapped, moving her arm before he could touch her.

How dared he talk of love? Of honour.

His anger was not directed at the disease that had killed his wife, but at the woman who had defied him to protect the baby she was carrying. If it had been a boy, she would have been celebrated, honoured. But his anger was eloquent testimony to the fact that a girl child was no compensation for the loss of his wife.

She'd thought him sympathetic, someone with whom she could converse on an equal footing, but her first terrified impression had been right. The man had the surface manners of a gentleman, but beneath the veneer his instincts were still those of a primitive tribal chieftain for whom women were no more than the expendable vessels who provided them with sons.

He grieved not for his wife, but for the son she had promised him.

CHAPTER FOUR

'LUCY?'

She forced herself to face him.

'Have you eaten well?' Unable to speak, she just nodded. 'Then I shall wash your hair.'

What?

How could he do that? One minute act like a relic of the Middle Ages, the next like some caring 'new' man?

Or had she misunderstood him? Misjudged him? Was his anger nothing more than a reflection of his pain that his wife had played on an Arab's desire for sons. Had not trusted him to accept her decision?

'If you'd rather not,' she said cautiously, 'perhaps Ameerah's nurse would help me.'

'Ameerah's nurse?'

'I saw her yesterday when she was chasing after your daughter.'

'I see.' His dark eyes glinted dangerously. 'You saw her and now you think I was lying to you when I told you there were no women in my house?'

She tried to deny it—the thought hadn't crossed her mind until he put it there—but the one word she needed seemed stuck in transit, somewhere between her brain and her mouth.

'Why would I do that?' he asked, taking her silence as affirmation.

She was not deceived by his reasonable tone, his bland expression. Too embarrassed to look at him, she simply shook her head. It was not enough and he reached across the table, hooked a finger beneath her chin, forcing her to meet his eyes.

Never had a touch been gentler or seemed more dangerous. The heat of it rippled through her. As a demonstration of her vulnerability, a warning of how totally she'd placed herself in his power, it had everything and, transfixed, she didn't move a muscle as his gaze drifted down to where the robe she was wearing over the nightgown had fallen open, unnoticed, as she'd eaten.

'You think that I am like some predator, perhaps, who takes a victim to his lair to feast upon at his leisure?'

'No!' She finally managed to deny it, released from stasis by the desperate need to reassure him that she'd never thought any such thing. The image he evoked was that of a leopard, or a bear. It did not suit him. If Hanif al-Khatib was a predator, he was a hawk, an eagle…

'No,' she repeated, but her denial was somewhat undermined by the nervous manner in which she clutched at the fragile silk, holding it together with one hand where it scooped low over her breast.

'Do you think that if I was the kind of man who preyed on helpless women,' he continued, the edge of his thumb so close to her cheek that she could feel the down rising to meet it, 'the presence of a dozen old women would stop me?'

'No! Yes!' At which point she realised that there wasn't a right answer to his question. That the only way to repair the unintended insult was to meet his gaze head on. Match his directness with a clear and unequivocal response.

'I assure you, Hanif bin Jamal bin Khatib al-

Khatib, that you have done nothing to make me feel uncomfortable or awkward. On the contrary.' He did not move. 'You have done nothing that a much loved wife could have reproached you for.'

For a moment the only thing that moved was the blood rushing to her cheeks. Then, with the slightest of bows, Hanif let his hand fall to his side.

'You are right to be careful, Lucy Forrester. You know nothing about me.'

She knew enough. Enough to judge him by his deeds rather than his words. To regret the unworthy thoughts that had filled her head, be grateful that she had not given them voice.

'I know that you saved my life, Hanif. That I am nothing to you, yet you have not spared any expense, begrudged one moment of your time, to care for me. It must have been out of the goodness of your heart,' she said as, desperate to convince him, she made a gesture that framed her bruised and swollen face. 'It certainly couldn't have been because of my beauty.'

He did not protest, attempt meaningless flattery, but said, 'The arrival of Ameerah and

Fathia, her nurse, was as unexpected as your own.' For unexpected read unwelcome, she thought. 'They did not arrive until yesterday afternoon and, as you have already noted, the old woman has her hands full.'

Hanif al-Khatib, she was almost certain, rarely felt the need to explain his actions. She understood instinctively that she had just been shown more than usual courtesy.

'She does not live with you?' she asked, as if they were having the most ordinary of conversations. Only the slightest tremble in her voice betrayed how intense the moment had been. 'Your daughter?'

'The garden offers no more than a pavilion for a pampered wife, a hunting lodge for her lord. There is nothing here for a child,' he said dismissively. 'Ameerah lives in the capital with her grandmother.' He rose to his feet and she thought the subject was closed, but then his mouth twisted in a parody of a smile. 'I suspect that when she heard I had taken in a young foreign woman, my mother despatched Ameerah to Rawdah al-'Arusah as a hostage to my honour. Or yours. I leave it to you to decide which,' he added, and the parody came close to approaching the real thing.

'If your mother could see the state of me,' Lucy assured him, wincing as her own attempt at a smile—just to demonstrate how it should be done—pulled at a cut on her lip, 'she wouldn't give the matter a moment's thought.'

'You are right, of course. Let us hope that Fathia will make time to call and reassure her.'

Oh, nice!

About to point out that a gentleman wouldn't have agreed with her, she thought better of it.

'I'm afraid that what should have been a simple rescue mission has caused you far more trouble than you could ever have bargained for.'

'*Mash'Allah,*' he said, handing her the crutches. Keeping close in case she needed help. But not, she noticed, making any attempt to assist her.

'*Mash'Allah,*' she said, repeating the words to herself as she swung herself back in through the open French windows, then, looking up at him, 'God's will?'

'You have been learning Arabic?' he enquired with interest.

'I bought one of those teach yourself language

CDs. I was...' She stopped. She had been planning to surprise Steve, determined to learn enough to help him run the business. 'I was hopeless,' she said.

'It's difficult to learn anything on your own, but in four weeks you can learn a great deal.'

'Four weeks?'

'Since you wanted to know how long it would take for your ankle to heal, I spoke with the doctor. He thought three or four weeks.'

'Oh, I see. Well, thank you, but I promise that I won't be imposing on your hospitality for more than a few days.'

'It is no imposition. And what will you do in England, alone in your cold, empty house? How will you manage to buy food, cook, take care of yourself?'

The one thing she wouldn't be doing was expecting help from the congregation of her grandmother's church. They had lost interest the minute they had discovered that there would be no more money. Besides, they all knew she was the devil's handmaid, born in wickedness, headed for hell.

'It's not cold,' she said.

'Everywhere in England is cold.' Apparently

taking her silence for assent, he continued, 'You will stay here until you are fully recovered, Lucy.' Then, almost as an afterthought, 'Or until your husband comes to find you.'

He picked up a chair and took it through to the bathroom, setting it with its back to the sink.

'Sit,' he said. 'I will try not to get you too wet,' he said, lifting the shower head from its holder and turning on the water.

She remained on her feet. 'You don't have to do this. I'm sure I could manage.'

He clearly did not think her protest worthy of a reply, but instead ran the water, adjusting the temperature. Or maybe it was a test of her trust. Of her sincerity when she'd assured him that he'd done nothing to offend her.

She sat down, did her best to scoop up her hair, lift it over the edge of the basin.

'Leave it. I will do it.'

She ignored him. She was not helpless. Another day, two at the most, and she would be on her way, however tempting it was to stay and be treated like a princess.

She had debts to deal with, a living to earn, a husband to divorce.

Han tucked a towel around her shoulders, then said, 'That is not too hot?' She shook her head without thinking and barely felt a twinge as warm water began to soak into her hair.

The lack of fuss with which he washed, then combed through her long difficult hair while it was slick with conditioner, left her in no doubt that he'd done this many times for a wife grown too weak to do it for herself.

The man seemed a muddle of contradictions, but then what did she know? She hadn't needed her grandmother's exhortations to purity to keep her chaste. There had been nothing about her to attract a man, even if she'd had the chance to meet one, until she'd inherited her grand-mother's house and Steve had turned up on the doorstep.

Hanif was a man so far outside her experience that she had no right to judge him, or the stan-dards by which he lived his life. Only the manner in which he treated her.

'I used to hate this,' she said afterwards, when they'd gone back out on to the balcony so that her hair could dry in the sun.

'Having your hair washed?'

'The washing wasn't so bad, but when I was a child my grandmother had this horrid scratchy comb and very little patience with tangles.'

'I will not hurt you,' he said, refusing to surrender the comb he'd brought with him but, taking infinite care not to hurt her, continued what he'd begun. 'It is unusual to see such long hair on a European woman.'

'Gran belonged to a dogmatic religious sect which believes it's a sin for women to cut their hair. She used to make me wear it in painfully tight plaits when I was little.'

'Plaits?'

She took a piece of hair and demonstrated what she meant.

'Oh, yes.'

'I once hacked them off with her kitchen scissors.' She used her fingers to show how she'd cut them as short as she could.

'She was angry?'

'She wasn't pleased,' Lucy admitted. She'd never told anyone about the beating she'd been given. Ghastly as her hair had looked, it had been less painful than the weekly agony with the wet tangles. The bruises had long faded before her hair had grown enough for plaits again and by then she'd taught herself to do it herself, putting it into a single French plait that was tight enough, unflattering enough, to keep her grandmother happy, grown up enough not to provoke cruel teasing at school. 'I was not a good child,' she said.

'Children are not supposed to be good. They are supposed to be children. You had no mother?'

'Somewhere.'

The truth slipped out before she could stop it. It wasn't her usual response. She usually told people that her mother had died when she was a baby. So much less painful than the truth. But she couldn't bring herself to lie to Han, who had a truly motherless child.

'I had—have—a mother somewhere. She abandoned me. Left me with her mother, ran away.' She didn't blame her for running. Only for leaving her behind. 'She was sixteen. Unmarried.'

It occurred to her that this would probably shock him. Maybe it had been her intention to shock him, show him just how special Noor had been. If her mother had had an ounce of his wife's compassion, love…

'Girls in the west are not protected by their fathers,' he said, apparently missing the comparison, or perhaps choosing to ignore it. 'They dress provocatively, go out unaccompanied. It is bound to happen.'

'Perhaps. Her father, my grandfather, died when she was fourteen. Maybe if he'd lived things would have been different.' Her grandmother might not have been drawn to such an intense religious experience. Her mother would not have been driven to rebel…

'He had no brothers?'

'Brothers?'

'Here,' he explained, 'when a man dies, his brother will take his family into his house. Care for his children. Stand in his place as husband.'

She frowned, turned to look up at him. 'Do you mean that literally? The husband bit? Even if he already has a wife?'

'A woman has needs,' he said. 'To be held, to have the comfort of the marriage bed if it is her wish. It is his duty.'

'I've never thought of it in quite that way before,' she admitted.

'You're blinkered by your own cultural traditions,' he said, clearly picking up more than a touch of irony in her response.

He had finished combing her hair and he moved her chair round so that the sun could finish drying it. 'You believe a man who does this is simply thinking of his own pleasure. That it demeans the woman.'

'To be wife number two?' She was absolutely sure it didn't raise her status, but thought she'd be well advised not to make comments on a subject she knew nothing about.

'The custom of taking more than one wife began as a way of caring for the widows of those fallen in battle,' he explained. 'It is not an easy thing for a man.'

'No?'

Maybe she didn't sound convinced.

'In the west you think of a man being served by two or three women. You find it salacious, titillating. The truth is that his responsibilities are onerous. Each wife has to be treated equally in all things. Give one woman a trinket, a dress, new furniture, and they must all have the same.'

'A man has to pay for his pleasure.'

'You are amused?'

'You expect me to feel sorry for a man who has three wives?'

'I was not seeking your sympathy, but your understanding of the reality. Have you any idea what would have happened to a woman left to fend for herself? To her children? There was no welfare state to care for them. They would have had to scrape a living any way they could. You need look no further than the evening news bulletin on your television to see the reality.'

'Oh.' She swallowed. 'I see.'

'It is rare for a man to take more than one wife now,' he said, as if to reassure her.

'Yes, well,' she said, rallying, 'I can see that in this consumer-led age it would be prohibitively expensive.'

'And physically exhausting.' And this time there was just a hint of a smile. 'Equality, as I said, in all things.'

'In England,' she said quickly, to cover her blushes, 'it has never been legal to have more than one wife at a time. Besides, my grandfather had no brothers. It was just me and my grandmother. And now she's dead too.'

'I am sorry to hear that.' Then, 'You have not looked for her?' he asked. 'Your mother?'

'Why would I do that?'

He shrugged.

'If she'd wanted to see me, Hanif, she knew where I was.' She'd dreamed of that. Of her mother swooping down to carry her off, taking her away to live with her in a warm house, dressing her in pretty clothes, giving her birthday parties at the local burger bar like the other kids. 'I was exactly where she left me.'

'Maybe she is too ashamed to come to you.'

'I don't believe she ever wasted a single thought on me,' she said.

He regarded her thoughtfully, but let it be. Her relief was a heartbeat too fast. 'And your husband?' he enquired. 'Does he not think of you? Wonder where you are?'

Even before the words left his mouth, Hanif wished them unsaid. He had offered her refuge without condition. Seeing her struggle to find some answer that would satisfy him only confirmed his opinion that she was in trouble. But while he would do whatever he could to extricate her from any legal problems she had in

Ramal Hamran, any difficulty between Lucy Forrester and her new husband was none of his business.

'Enough,' he said, standing up. 'The sun is too hot for your fair skin. You need to be inside where it is cool, resting.'

'I thought it would be hotter,' she said, gratefully seizing on the change of subject. 'When I arrived at the airport it seemed worse.'

'The humidity at the coast can be unpleasant at this time of year. It is higher here and cooler, but you must still take care. The breeze from the mountains deceives. You do not need sunburn to add to your discomfort.'

The balcony was wide and shaded, but even so her skin was flushed with the heat. Or maybe, he thought, it was guilt.

It did not matter.

He handed her the crutches and said, 'Come, this way.' And forcing himself to turn away, leave her to it, he walked further along the balcony, opening the French windows into the sitting room.

'Zahir! I have a job for you.'

'Excellency?'

'You were given Lucy Forrester's belongings? At the hospital?'

'Yes, Excellency, but they were beyond saving. The nurses cut them off her.'

'Was there any jewellery?'

'I have the bag in my office.'

'This is everything?' Hanif asked, when the envelope containing only a wrist-watch, no longer working, had been opened.

'Was there something in particular you were looking for?'

'I want you to go back to the hospital and make sure nothing was missed. Find the nurse who admitted her if you can and ask if there was a ring.'

'Yes, sir.'

'And while you're in Rumaillah you can buy clothes to replace those she lost in the crash.'

'Me?' The word was little more than a squeak.

'You can take the sizes from these,' Hanif said, indicating the ruins of the clothes she'd been wearing.

'You're asking me to shop for women's clothes? Women's underwear?'

'The duties of an aide are onerous,' he agreed. Then, taking pity on him, he said, 'Maybe one

of your female relatives would do it for you if
you asked politely.'

'You are joking! Ask my sisters to help me buy
underwear for a woman? I'd have my ears boxed.'

'Then it would appear that you are in for an uncomfortable time, either way.'

'On the other hand, if I explained it was a commission for you, they would fall over themselves
to be helpful. In fact, that would work very well.
They can shop while I take a closer look at this
tour company. See what kind of an outfit they
are.'

'How will you approach them?'

'There are sand-surfing trips run every day,
with evening banquets in the desert to round
things off. I've still got the clothes I wore when
I was a student in the States so I can pass as a
visitor and it will give me a chance to talk to the
people who work there.' Zahir's eagerness suggested it was the chance to get away, be with
young people, rather than the investigation that
excited him. 'I'll arrange for the results of my
sisters' raid on the mall to be sent back on the helicopter.'

'You seem to have it all worked out. Very well,

Zahir, but be careful what you say and do not mention Lucy Forrester's name.'

Lucy thought she heard the sound of a helicopter flying low and peered out of the window, hoping to see whether it was leaving or landing.

As she reached for her crutches, determined, despite Han's order to rest, that she would go outside and take a closer look, she spotted Ameerah peeping round the door. The child immediately ducked out of sight, but didn't run, and when Lucy called, '*Marhaban,* Ameerah,' her response was a giggle.

'*Ismy,* Lucy,' she said. 'My name is Lucy.'

'Lucy,' the child repeated, still not showing herself.

Lucy did not respond and after a moment Ameerah's face edged around the door. Her eyes were bright with mischief, her hair an untidy tangle of long dark curls with ribbons that had once been tied in bows but were now trailing loose.

When she was sure that Lucy was not going to shout at her or reach for the hand bell to summon her nurse, she eased herself around the door and into the room.

Her feet were bare and muddy, but she was wearing an exquisite cream silk dress, the kind worn by small princesses in story books. Once pin-tucked and perfect, it was now a mess, the hem soaking wet and coated with green algae as if it had been trailed through a pond and sporting the kind of jagged tear that suggested it had got into a fight with the branch of a tree and lost.

She'd obviously given her nurse the slip again. A handful indeed. And, with no one of her own age to play with, probably bored out of her mind.

Trawling through what she could remember of the language CD, Lucy was unable to come up with anything to fit the occasion. Instead she shifted herself to make more room on the day bed and patted the space beside her.

Ameerah didn't take up the invitation, but instead pressed herself against the wall and edged herself along it until she reached the safety of an elegant loveseat, upholstered in rose silk. Perching herself on that, feet swinging, she regarded Lucy with an intense, unblinking stare.

Lucy made no effort to coax her nearer, nor did she smile. Her reward for her patience came when Ameerah lifted her skirt and pointed to a colourful bruise on her shin.

'Ouch!' Lucy said sympathetically.

Ameerah nodded, then pointed first to her own eye, then at Lucy and said. 'Ouch!'

Lucy laughed. '*Nam,* Ameerah,' she said. 'Yes. A very big ouch.'

Encouraged, Ameerah slid from the seat and came a little closer, her interest apparently snagged by the splint Lucy was wearing. She looked at it, touched it very gently, then held out one of her own slender little arms, pointing at a small scar.

Lucy responded with a sympathetic expression, sucking air through her teeth in an internationally understood message of sympathy before asking, somewhat helplessly, in English, 'How did you hurt yourself, Ameerah?'

The child responded in a rush of Arabic, speaking so quickly that Lucy couldn't pick out a single word. When she held up her hands and shook her head, Ameerah responded by miming a break so graphically, with sound effects, that Lucy clapped her hand over her mouth.

Apparently delighted with the effect she'd

produced, the child laughed, then, turning as she heard her name being called, dropped to her knees and scuttled beneath the day bed.

CHAPTER FIVE

AMEERAH'S nurse paused in the doorway, looked at Lucy and said, 'Pardon, *assayyidah*. I am seeking the child. Ameerah.'

Lucy said, 'If I see her, *assayyidah,* I will ring the bell.' Then, lifting a finger to her lips, she indicated Ameerah's hiding place and, using the same signs—patting the space beside her—made it clear that she was welcome to stay for a while.

The woman smiled, nodded, indicated that she'd be within call and disappeared, presumably to have a much needed break.

Once she was gone, Lucy leaned down, lifted the drapes that hung to the floor and said, 'Okay, Ameerah, you can come out now.'

The child's head appeared; she looked around, up at Lucy, who nodded, then, with a huge smile on her face, she crawled out and bounced up beside her.

'Lucy,' she said, touching her hand.

'Ameerah,' Lucy replied, gently touching the child's cheek. And they both smiled.

Then Ameerah pointed to the jug on the table beside her. '*Mai,*' she said.

For a moment she thought the child was saying 'my', then realized she was asking for water. She poured some into the glass. '*Tafazzal...*' she said, offering it to her. Please have. Ameerah giggled, repeating the word several times before taking the glass. Then, as soon as she'd finished her drink, she wriggled down, put the glass on the table and ran to the door.

'Oh, I see. Cupboard love, is it?' Lucy said, laughing.

Ameerah turned and, with a neat curtsey that belied her untidy appearance, said, '*Shukran,* Lucy.'

'*Afwan,* Ameerah. *Ma'as salamah.*'

The child laughed, calling something back to her as she ran off.

Lucy reran the words in her head until she could make sense of the sounds, match them to the CD she'd spent so much time listening to. 'Oh, right.' She laughed. 'See you later.'

She rang the bell and, when the nurse reappeared, indicated the direction her charge had taken.

Han heard Lucy's bell. The sound surprised him. He had come to the conclusion that she would do anything, even crawl on her hands and knees to the bathroom, rather than ring for help and in another five minutes he would have looked in on her to see if she needed anything.

Maybe, he thought with more than a touch of amusement, beneath that reticent exterior there was an unsuspected 'princess' trying to break free.

Or maybe she was in real trouble. He wasted no more time in speculation.

Lucy, however, was sitting quietly, a small wistful smile lifting the corners of her mouth. It disappeared the minute she caught sight of him.

'Oh... Han.'

'You seem surprised to see me, Lucy. You did ring?'

'Yes, but—'

'But?'

But she hadn't rung for him, that much was clear.

He could almost see the cogs whirring around in her head as she struggled for some explanation.

'—but I didn't expect you to be so quick. You said someone would come and find you. I thought it would take longer.'

'This is not a palace, Lucy. It is, as I told you, nothing more than a small pavilion. A place to spend the hot summer months. What you would call a holiday cottage.'

'Only in the way that Balmoral or Camp David is a holiday cottage,' she replied. Then, apparently unsure whether he'd ever heard of either of them, she explained, 'Balmoral is Queen Elizabeth's Scottish home. Our royal family spend their holidays there.'

He didn't tell her that he'd not only heard of it, but had been a guest there on more than one occasion. Instead he said, 'You mock me, Lucy. Rawdah al-'Arusah has no more than twelve rooms.'

'Twelve. Is that all?'

Sarcasm, too. Lucy Forrester was recovering fast. 'Fifteen, at the most,' he assured her. He discounted all but the major rooms.

'It seems very grand to me.' She gestured

around at the exquisite hand-painted tiles, the rugs, the furniture upholstered in rich silk. 'It is certainly beautiful.'

'It was built as a setting for a princess. The only man allowed within its walls would have been her husband.'

She blushed. 'Excuse me? Are you telling me that this was a harem?'

'I suspect what you mean by that word and the reality are so far apart as to render it meaningless. This was a citadel. A place apart where no one could come unless she permitted it.'

'Not even her husband?'

'Not even her husband.'

'Really?' Her surprise amused him. 'So where did he stay?'

'There is a lodge, out of sight of the pavilion, where he stayed with his men, as I did myself until Noor became ill and I took a suite of rooms for myself to be near her.'

Something knotted in Lucy's stomach, a feeling she could not describe. But in her head she saw the beautiful Noor summoning her husband to her. Dressed in silk, her hair polished and glowing, she would have prepared every-

thing to please him. She would have offered him
food, made him laugh, made him wait as she
drove him wild with desire…

'Lucy? Are you all right?'

She came to with a start, swallowed. 'Yes.
Fine. Really.' Then, 'You stayed here. Afterwards.'

'It is peaceful. I do not disturb my family.'

They worried about him, she thought. He
stayed here so that they shouldn't see him
grieve…

'What do you find to do all day?'

'I take my hawks into the desert to exercise
them. Visit with local tribes to ensure they have
everything they need. And the garden had been
neglected for a long time. It needs care.'

'You're restoring it?'

'Returning it to what it was? It can never be that,
but some of the irrigation systems are showing the
signs of age; if they are left to crumble the garden
will eventually die. And my library is here, so you
see I have more than enough to keep me occupied.'

'Even without having the additional worry of
stupid women doing their best to kill themselves
on your doorstep.'

'The life of one woman is more important than a hundred gardens, a lifetime of study.'

'Study?' In a moment she was all remorse. 'You were working? Just now? I'm so sorry to have disturbed you—'

'I am translating the work of one of our poets into French and English. Scarcely a matter of urgency,' he said, dismissing what would be a life's work with a gesture.

'Then you too must be a poet.' Before he could deny it, she said, 'It is not just a matter of translating the words, but the meaning, the voice, the rhythm.'

'You speak as someone who knows the problems.'

'I was hoping to study French literature at university.'

'This did not happen?'

'My grandmother thought university was a haven of sin. That I would be corrupted by it. When I refused to obey her and stay at home she became so angry that she had a heart attack and then a stroke. There was no one but me to nurse her.'

'She paid a high price for getting her own way.'

'We both did.'

'Is there anything to prevent you from resuming your studies now?'

'I thought of it, but then Steve Mason turned up on my doorstep, so once again university has become the impossible dream it always was.'

'Because you are married? This Steve Mason is the man you married?'

'Yes. You know him?'

'No. I'm simply surprised that you do not use his name.'

'It's a long story, Han, and you have work to do.'

'Even poets take coffee breaks,' he said, but the last thing he wanted to talk about was her marriage, her husband. Instead he turned to the telephone beside a small love seat and immediately saw the wet, muddy smear on the edge of one of the cushions. So the mystery of the bell was explained. Ameerah had been here again and, protective of the child, Lucy had not been prepared to betray her.

He asked for coffee to be sent up, then turned and sat down facing his guest. 'So, you are rested, Lucy Forrester and impatient to see the garden?'

Startled by the abrupt change of subject, she said, 'I'm sorry?'

'I assume you summoned me to take you for a walk.'

Lucy had been wondering how she was going to save Ameerah from the consequences of her trespass into the forbidden area of the pavilion. She wasn't exactly keen to tell Han the sorry tale of her marriage either and, tossed a verbal lifeline, she seized it gratefully.

'You're right. I crave fresh air. A book. A shady seat.' Then, because it had been bothering her, she said, 'Can I ask you something?'

'What do you wish to know?'

'How did you find my address? In England. I know my memory, in the aftermath of the accident, became a little muddled, but I can't recall giving it at the hospital. Or insurance details, come to that.' He didn't immediately answer and, certain she was right to press it, she said, 'Everything was destroyed, you said.'

'It was,' he assured her, then turned to welcome the arrival of a servant with coffee. He dismissed the boy, served her himself and offered her a plate containing small sticky cakes.

'They are very good,' he said. 'The almonds are grown here.'

Lucy did not have a sweet tooth, but she took one and tasted it. 'Delicious,' she said politely. 'And the honey? Is that produced here too?'

He glanced at her a little sharply, as if suspecting that she was teasing him, then said, 'I did not say; I thought you might think me boastful.'

'On the contrary, I believe you to be the most modest of men,' she said, resting the cake in the saucer of the coffee cup he'd placed beside her.

It was true. His robes were plain, dark, simply cut, without adornment, and the *keffiyeh* he'd been wearing when he'd rescued her was the kind worn by desert tribesmen rather than those made from fine white voile and worn with the elaborate gilded camel halters favoured by the rich.

Then, persisting, 'You didn't ask me for my address, Hanif. Yet you knew it.'

'You were in shock, in pain, when we arrived at the hospital and you were not making a great deal of sense. We needed to find your friends, so I had my aide make enquiries, first, as I told you, with the company whose vehicle you were driving and then, when that proved a dead end, he spoke to the immigration department. Fortunately the officers on duty when you arrived remembered you.'

'I find that hard to believe.'

'Your hair, I understand, made a considerable impression.'

'Oh.' She normally wore it in a French plait or coiled in a bun to keep it out of the way, but in her agitation, her rush to get to the airport, her fingers had refused to co-operate and she'd simply dragged it back from her face, fastened it at the nape with a clip, leaving it to hang loose down her back. Then, 'Your aide?'

'Zahir al-Khatib. A cousin. He's in Rumaillah this morning.'

'Making further enquiries?'

'Replacing your wardrobe. Or, rather, delegating the task to one of his sisters.'

Lucy suspected this was a distraction, tossed into the conversation to avoid more questions. No doubt she was supposed to exclaim with horror, tell him that he could not do that, but she didn't waste her breath. If he'd decided she needed clothes, then clothes she would have. And, unless she was prepared to travel home in his late wife's nightdress, she was going to have to accept them. But not as charity.

'I did have travel insurance,' she said. 'It will cover the replacement of my clothes.'

'Are you sure? I suspect that if they discover you were driving a stolen vehicle when you lost your possessions, you might find the company disinclined to pay out.'

Oh, good grief, she hadn't thought of that. 'If, as you say, Bouheira Tours deny all knowledge of the vehicle, that shouldn't prove a problem. I will pay for my clothes, Han.'

Lucy saw him bite back an instinctive response.

He must know that even in Britain it would be inappropriate to buy clothes for another man's wife. Here, she suspected, such liberties might get a man killed, although the truth was that he'd gone way beyond any such barrier even before he'd removed her from the hospital; the fact he hadn't known she was married would be no excuse.

But he was safe enough. She doubted Steve would come looking for satisfaction—not unless he thought there was money in it.

'There were traveller's cheques too,' she said. Not many. She could not afford to be extravagant. Actually she couldn't even afford to be cheap... 'And my return ticket. Will the airline issue a replacement?'

'If you give me what details you can remember, Zahir will deal with it for you.'

'The same Zahir who was able to bypass all red tape and get my address from immigration? He must be a handy man to have around.'

'The population of Ramal Hamrah is small,' Han said. 'The immigration officers will have known him.'

'Is that enough? I can't imagine being an acquaintance of an immigration officer would get you access to that kind of information in England.'

'This is not England. This is Ramal Hamrah.'

A country rich in oil, with a thriving offshore banking industry and a growing tourist sector. A very foreign country. One where marriages were arranged, where a man could take more than one wife if he had the wealth and the stamina, and where daughters had no value.

'So if they knew your cousin, it follows that they would know you.' His shrug was imperceptible. 'Why does the name Khatib seem so familiar?'

'The Khatibs are an old Ramal Hamrah family.'

That didn't explain it, so she came at it another way. She had already learned the importance of names. That a first-born son was named for his grandfather…

'You are not your father's oldest son,' she said, 'or your name would be Khatib bin Jamal bin whatever.'

'That is the name of my oldest brother,' he confirmed, but offering her nothing more.

He wasn't exactly hindering her, but she sensed a mystery, that she was missing something.

'If I were a Ramal Hamrah, if I lived here, your extended name would be enough to tell me who you are and your place within the family.'

'I am the third son of Jamal,' he said. Then, apparently taking pity on her, 'Perhaps, if I show you a photograph of my father, you will understand.'

Family photographs? Her heart skipped a beat… 'I should like to understand.'

He summoned the *farraish* who was sitting

cross-legged in the hallway waiting to take away the tray when they were finished, gave him an order. It seemed for ever before he returned, not with a photograph, as she'd expected, not even a portrait, but with a small piece of coloured paper, folded in two. He offered it to Han, who indicated that he should give it to Lucy.

He offered it with both hands, bowing low, taking care not to look directly at her, before backing out of the room.

'It's a Ramal Hamrah bank note,' she said, confused. 'A hundred riyals.'

Han said nothing. Obviously she'd missed something. She turned it over and that was when she saw the engraving of the Emir.

'Oh,' she said, finally remembering where she'd seen the name before—on the website when she had been researching Ramal Hamrah. 'I rather wish I hadn't asked that question. Why didn't you tell me straight away?'

'Because it was not important. I've only told you now because you pressed the matter and I wished to reassure you. Zahir was only able to learn your name so easily because he was asking for me. No one else will find you.'

'No one else is looking,' she said. 'I'm sorry, Han, but Steve isn't about to turn up and take me off your hands.'

For a moment she thought he might question her about that. About Steve.

'In that case it is even more important to assure you that you are safe here. You will be cared for. As soon as you are ready, Zahir will take you to your embassy so that you can arrange for new papers and, when you are fit, able to manage on your own, he will make whatever arrangements for your return home or, if you wish, your continued stay.'

'Why? Why are you doing this?' She didn't wait for one of his enigmatic replies, waving it aside before he could tell her that it was traditional courtesy to a stranger in need. This was more than that. 'You could have sorted all that out at long distance, Han…' Her voice wobbled on his name. The man was the son of the Emir, local royalty, and she was talking to him as if he were someone she'd known all her life. 'You could have left it to Zahir. Or even handed me over to the embassy.'

'Yes,' he agreed, 'I could have done that.'

'So why did you bring me here? You did not have to take me in, look after me yourself.'

'Maybe,' he said, after a silence that seemed endless. 'Maybe I needed to do it.'

Lucy opened her mouth, then closed it again and not just because the question that had rushed to her lips—*Why?*—seemed insensitive, intrusive. As his forehead creased in a frown she sensed that his response had been in the nature of self-revelation and for once this desert lord—and her instincts, so lacking where Steve had been concerned, had not let her down this time—appeared almost vulnerable.

Instead of challenging him, she turned away to give him time to gather himself. Picking up the cake, she concentrated her entire attention on it.

Eventually he stood up and left the room and the breath she'd been holding left her body in a rush. Her hand was shaking as she let it drop to her lap.

'Ready?'

She looked up. Han had returned with a lightweight wheelchair.

'No,' she protested. 'I can walk.'

'It is too far. We will take your crutches and

once we have reached the summer house you can explore the garden, if you wish.'

'Are you sure?' she asked, feeling horribly guilty, and not just because she'd lied about wanting to sit in the garden, although actually, now the possibility was offered, she couldn't think of anything she'd like more. But she didn't believe he'd brought a wheelchair from the hospital for her convenience; this was a state-of-the-art machine and clearly it had been used by his wife when she'd become too sick to walk.

She knew that everything he was doing for her must be bringing back dreadful memories, but she couldn't say that.

'If you're sure,' she said feebly. 'I don't want to disrupt your work.'

'The west has waited four centuries to read the beauty of Abu Jafr's words—another hour or two will make no difference.'

To protest further would embarrass them both and she surrendered, accepting a hand so that she could move from the couch to the chair, sweeping her hair to one side as she sat down.

'I don't suppose Zahir will think to buy hairpins, will he?' she asked. 'I usually wear it tied back. Did the hospital give you my things? There should be a large clip amongst them.'

Han knew there was not, but even if he hadn't looked through her pitifully few belongings he would still have known. When he'd found her, Lucy's hair had been tumbled loose about her like a shawl.

'There was nothing salvageable.'

'Well, that's it,' she said, with the air of someone who had made an irrevocable decision. 'I'm going to get it cut the minute I get home. Really short.'

'But why?' he asked. He could understand why a child might cut off hated plaits, but for a grown woman to deprive herself of such glory seemed perverse.

'It gets in the way. It's a nuisance. I meant to have it cut right after my grandmother's funeral, in one of those flirty little bobs,' she said, flicking at it. She'd wanted to do it before the funeral, to shock all those miserable old biddies who'd helped make her life a misery until she'd been old enough to refuse to do more than deliver her grandmother to the church door and collect her after the service.

'Your grandmother could not have stopped

you from doing what you wanted with it these last ten years, surely?'

'No. She could not have stopped me; in fact, she expected me to cut it.' Just as she'd expected to be abandoned, to have revisited on her all the misery she'd dished out over the years. 'Was waiting for it. Instead, once I had control of the housekeeping money, I bought good shampoo, conditioner, a soft-toothed comb. Wore it loose.'

'To torment her?'

'I told you I was not good.'

'So you did.' He lifted a handful of her hair and let it fall slowly before her eyes in a shimmer of palest gold. 'I hope you'll forgive me if I suggest that you did it a little for yourself too.'

Her lips parted on a protest. He didn't know what he was talking about.

The words didn't come.

'I will find some pins for you,' he said, tugging on the leather cord tying his own hair back, looping it around hers in a bow to keep it from falling over her face. 'In the mean-time, perhaps this will help.'

Neither of them said a word as they descended in the small, ornate lift that took them to the ground floor, or as he wheeled her through blue-tiled cloistered arches and out into the dappled shade of the willows and Judas trees that overhung the sparkling rill of water. But as the warmth wrapped itself around them like a comfort blanket, Lucy sighed with pleasure.

'You're right, Han,' she said, glancing up at him. 'In comparison with this, England does seem cold and uninviting. Did you spend much time there?'

'School, university,' he said. 'Do not misunderstand me. Your country is a place of great beauty and I loved it. But the rain…'

'I know, but I'm afraid all that greenery comes at a price.'

'At first it was a novelty,' he said, encouraged by her laughter. 'I ran outside just to feel it on my face.'

'I'll bet you soon got over that.'

He parked her in the shade of an extensive rose-covered summer house set beside a large informal pool and placed a small leather-bound book on the table beside her.

She picked it up, opened it.

'Some of the translated poems of the Persian

poet, Hafiz,' he said. 'He uses the imagery of the garden to express love in all its forms.'

'I can't think of anything more perfect to read in such a place.' She glanced up from the page. 'You know you don't have to stay, Han.'

No. He did not have to stay, but for once in his life he was in no hurry to return to his study. To sit beside Lucy while she read the poems of Hafiz, share lunch with her, was a far more appealing prospect.

'I have your book, the garden,' she said. 'I've disturbed you enough. Please don't let me keep you from your work.'

She did more than disturb him. She stirred him.

Injured, unhappy, she still brought with her a breath of something rare, something forgotten. It was anger that had brought her flying to Ramal Hamrah on the heels of her husband, passion that had driven her to steal a vehicle, risk everything to chase him across the desert.

He almost thought that if he held her, touched his mouth to hers, took in the breath as it left her body, he would feel it too, would begin to breathe again, feel again.

'Go,' she said, laughing, opening the book, glancing at the pages as she sought some word, some phrase to catch her eye. 'I promise I won't do anything stupid, like falling in the water.'

It was her laughter, the echo of other, infinitely precious days, that brought him to his senses. This was where he'd sat with Noor, reading to her as the child she loved more than him sucked the life out of her, knowing that with every breath she was slipping away from him, knowing that no amount of money, power, could save her...

'With that guarantee, I will leave you in peace,' he said abruptly.

Lucy waited until he was out of sight before she lifted her head from the book. She couldn't believe how hard it had been to send him away. How the presence of a man she barely knew could make her feel so precious, so special.

But, no matter what Steve had done, how he had betrayed her, she was not free to feel this way. Even so, she could not stop herself from looking back along the path he'd taken to the pavilion. The air was filled with the scents of herbs where he'd brushed past them as they spilled over on to the warm stones.

A dragonfly hovered, darted over the water, and still she looked, half expecting him to return.

Instead, after a while, a young servant came down the path, bringing jugs of water and juice. Her crutches too, in case she wanted to explore. He plugged in a telephone and set it beside her. Finally, he offered her a note written on thick cream paper.

The hand was bold, strong, the words brief.

Lucy, if you need to make calls home, please just lift the receiver and press 0 and you will have a line—the international code for the United Kingdom is 44. Leave out the first 0 in the number. If you need anything else, just press 1. Han.

She sighed.

She really should call the estate agent she'd instructed to sell the house. Tell them to put it back on the market.

It had been her intention to use the money to buy something small, modern, with central heating and hot water whenever she wanted it.

She should have done it before she'd left on

this wild goose chase, but she'd still been fooling herself that it was all some kind of mix-up. Some mistake.

Then she'd walked into the office of Bouheira Tours and had come face to face with reality.

There had been no mistake. No point in putting off the inevitable. The money would be needed to pay off the debts Steve had run up in her name and the sooner the better.

She should call her next door neighbour too. She had a key; the estate agents would need that.

And the insurance company to make a claim for medical expenses—there must have been medical expenses—and for her luggage.

And the bank. She'd assured them she was sorting everything out. They wouldn't be patient.

Han sat at his desk, the translation he'd been working on ignored. For a while he'd been in danger of forgetting the torment of the days he'd spent with Noor, knowing that there was nothing he could do, seeing the fear grow behind her brave smile.

To even smile at another woman was a betrayal of her courage. To hold Lucy, the way he'd held

Noor, as he'd helped her walk to the shower, to wash and comb her hair, to feel the heat of her body through the finest silk, her curves yield to his hands, to respond to her closeness as a man, enclosed so intimately with a woman, must always respond.

He did not understand why he felt this way. There was nothing to attract him. Her face was bruised, her eyes half closed, her lips puffy and cracked…

Yet, even now, he was waiting for the phone to ring, longing for the phone to ring, wanting her to need him so that he could go to her.

Disgusted with himself, he abandoned his translation, deliberately walked away from his desk, determined to visit the stables, the mews. His animals were well looked after, but he should still have seen for himself that his horse had suffered no ill effects from the headlong rush down the *jebel* as he'd ridden to Lucy Forrester's aid. He should spend time with his hawks.

He had scarcely left the pavilion before the sound of laughter reached him, brought him to a halt. Who was she talking to? Who had she called? Was it the neglectful husband who brought such joy to her?

He couldn't get the picture out of his mind of the reckless way she'd been driving the 4x4, racing across the desert. Had she been flying to Steve Mason, or running away from him?

It shouldn't matter. She belonged to another man.

Then he heard the laughter again and, unable to help himself, he moved closer, standing in the deep shade of a gnarled and ancient cypress tree watching as, completely absorbed in each other, Lucy Forrester and the child he had never been able to bring himself to touch, hold, acknowledge, played the simplest of games together.

'...chin,' Lucy said, touching her chin, then taking Ameerah's hand and holding it there.

'Chin,' Ameerah repeated, then touched her own face, said the word in Arabic, before taking Lucy's hand to her own face and waiting for her to repeat it.

They moved on. Hair, hand, elbow—first in English, then in Arabic.

Ameerah made Lucy say 'elbow' over and

over, repeating it herself with a long roll on the
'l'. There was much laughter.

It was a scene of such innocence, such simple
joy, that he had to reach out and grasp one of the
twisted trunks of the tree as raw pain threatened
to overwhelm him.

CHAPTER SIX

LUCY wasn't sure when she first became aware of Hanif, of a deeper shadow beneath the ancient cypress tree. She sensed him before she saw him. Felt the air shimmer with some powerful emotion that swept over her, raising the hairs on the back of her neck.

It took every ounce of effort not to look up, stop herself from turning to include him in their game, keep her attention totally focused on Ameerah.

His little girl had sought her out, bored with her own company, with a nurse who could not keep up, and it should have been the most natural thing in the world for Hanif to join them, pick up the child, hug her, tease her a little.

She had never had that for herself, but had seen it outside school, had seen other children scooped up, cuddled, their pictures admired by loving parents. She'd been the one alone, then, outside; she knew how it felt and she wanted to turn to him, stretch out a hand, say, Come and play. But he wasn't a child. He had chosen to cut himself off from this scrap of a girl who, with her dark hair and eyes, shining smile, represented everything that he had lost.

It wasn't just grief that kept him here in Rawdah al-'Arusah, shut away from life. It was anger too. And perhaps more than a little guilt that, unable to save her mother, he could not find a place in his heart for the child for whom she'd sacrificed herself.

Despite the fact that this was his home, it was his dark and solitary figure which was standing on the outside, looking in, unable to make that first step, breach the barriers.

Hanif had implied that the child had been sent as some kind of chaperon, but it occurred to her that his desperate mother may have hoped that a woman, someone the lively and curious Ameerah would be drawn to, might, in some way, be the catalyst who would draw them together.

It would be small enough repayment for all

he'd done for her, but Hanif al-Khatib was a complex and sophisticated man. He would see right through an invitation to Come and play.

'Are you hungry?' she asked Ameerah. '*Aakul?*' She caught the little girl to her, rubbed her tummy. 'What would you like to eat? Chicken? Hummus? Some of that good goat's cheese?'

The child giggled, wriggled around in her arms to face her, not to pull away.

'You know, what we really need is some paper and pencils,' Lucy said. 'Then you could draw me a picture of what you'd like.'

Han knew she'd seen him.

There had been no change in her manner and yet he sensed an awareness in her; Ameerah was no longer the sole focus of her attention. She was no longer entirely lost in the game.

And having been seen, he could not just walk away. He should have stuck to his original plan, gone to the stables; now he had no choice but to join them.

He crossed to the summer house, ready to send Ameerah back to her nurse, insist that Lucy return to her room to rest. But Fathia, the old woman who had once been his own nurse and as dear to him as his mother, was there too, dozing on a sofa, while Lucy occupied the child.

He didn't know what his mother had been thinking of, sending her out to al-'Arusah. She had long since retired and should be sitting in the shade of her own garden, being cared for by her own family, not chasing around after a three-year-old. Ameerah needed a young nanny, someone with the energy to keep up with her.

Someone to amuse her, play with her, as Lucy had been doing. But to say so would give his mother the opportunity to tell him it was time he did something about it.

Since Fathia was here, he had no option but to pick up the phone and, doing his best to ignore the way Ameerah shrank nervously back against Lucy, hiding herself in the folds of her robe, trying to make herself as inconspicuous as possible, he gave orders to the kitchen to send food out for the three of them.

'Lunch will be brought out here for you,' he said, turning to Lucy. Then, obliquely, 'Don't tire yourself.'

'I'm fine.' As he moved to leave, she said, 'Han? Won't you stay and join us?'

'No.' The sound of her laughter had drawn him here and if she'd been alone he would have been tempted. More than tempted. Ameerah's presence had worked a charm, serving to remind him of reality, but, aware that he had been abrupt, he gave the slightest of bows and said, 'I regret that I have things to see to in the stables.'

From the depths of the sofa Fathia snorted, her voice following him as he walked away. 'Going by the scenic route, were you?' she said, taking the kind of liberties permitted an old woman who'd held him as a helpless baby.

Since she spoke in Arabic, Lucy did not understand what she said or, worse, what she'd implied, while he took the only course open to him and resorted to diplomatic deafness. But, before he went to the stables, he returned to his study. Searching through a cupboard for coloured pencils, he found a box of pastels. He brushed the dust from the lid, opened it. They were old, worn from use. They had been given to him by his father one summer when he'd had to stay in the capital on affairs of state and couldn't come with them to al-'Arusah. He'd used them, had drawn pictures to send his father every day. Had kept and treasured them.

It was a small victory. Hanif had been listening. He hadn't stayed, but he had responded to his daughter's needs. They ate, played the finger games she'd learned when helping at summer play camps, used the paper and pastels he'd sent with a servant to draw pictures, while Fathia watched contentedly from the sofa.

But as the sun came round, grew too hot for comfort, Fathia summoned Ameerah, explaining, 'It is time for her to sleep. You, too, *assayyidah*. You must go inside now, rest until the evening.'

Lucy was flagging in the heat and she made no protest when Fathia insisted on wheeling her inside, settling her comfortably on the day bed, before dragging a reluctant Ameerah away for her afternoon nap.

'I'll see you later, sweetheart,' she said. *'Bashufak bahdain.'*

Ameerah broke away from Fathia to thrust one of the pictures she'd drawn into Lucy's hand, scampering shyly away before she could look at it.

It was a simple enough picture, the kind that any three-year-old might draw. Three stick people. A tall daddy with a straight mouth, a smaller smiling mummy and a little girl with a smile that reached from ear to ear.

As Lucy held it, certain for a moment that her heart would break for the child, she heard someone coming and she quickly folded the drawing and tucked it inside the book of poems, out of sight. Then, heart beating so fast that she was sure he must hear, she waited. But it wasn't Hanif. It was a young servant bringing her fresh water, a small bowl of dates. He bowed himself out and, after a moment, when her heart had returned to something like its normal pace, she sank back against the pillow and closed her eyes.

When she woke the sun was low. She yawned, stretched, sat up and saw that every surface of the room appeared to be covered by pastel-coloured boxes with famous names upon them. The kind of glossy carriers that only came from the most expensive stores.

Hanif had been there while she'd slept, she realized, a Santa in Sheikh's clothing.

Excited by the prospect of new clothes, she picked up the crutches, got to her feet and began to explore the contents. Silk underwear, designer label shirts, beautifully cut trousers, as well as more traditional clothes. There was a *shalwar kameez,* embroidered kaftans and wide silk chiffon scarves. More shoes than she could wear in a year, exquisite handbags. She touched one that had a Chanel logo on the fastening and knew without having to be told that this was the real thing.

And it wasn't just clothes.

Whoever had been given the task of replacing her belongings had taken the job seriously. There was every kind of personal toiletry, make-up, a hairbrush, pins, combs to keep her hair in place.

She subsided on to the satin love seat, holding a wrought silver pin against her breast. Had he remembered? Called someone, asked them to be sure and bring something to hold her hair in place?

She looked about her in desperation. It was all so beautiful.

So expensive.

She'd told him that she would pay for the clothes she needed, but she should have explained that her travel insurance would only cover the most basic of chain store buys. She wouldn't be able to pay for these if she worked for the rest of her life.

She had to explain. Tell him. Now. And she set the silver pin on the table, picked up her crutches and made her slow, careful way along the wide hallway to his study.

Hanif was sitting with his back to the open door, his gaze fixed on some distant horizon far beyond the darkening skyline. She hesitated in the doorway, unwilling to disturb his reverie.

'Will I never persuade you to ring the bell, Lucy Forrester?' he asked, without turning around.

'Not in a thousand years,' she assured him. 'I'm not an invalid. Besides, I need the exercise.'

'Always an answer.'

'That's what you get when you ask a question,' she pointed out.

He spun around in his chair. 'What is it? What do you want from me?'

To be back in her room, she thought, taking a step back, stumbling awkwardly.

'No…' The word escaped him as if, against his better judgement, he wanted her to stay and, before she could regain her balance, he was beside her, helping her towards a deep sofa. 'Please. Tell me what I can do for you.'

She regarded the sofa with misgiving. He was not going to be happy with her and at least while she was on her feet she could walk away. Sunk into the depths of those cushions, she would be trapped. But he waited, hand at her arm, until she lowered herself carefully on to the edge of the seat.

'Can I offer you something? Tea? Coffee?'

She shook her head. 'I just wanted to talk to you about the clothes you've bought me. They're going to have to go b-back…' she began, but his forbidding expression brought her stuttering to a halt.

'You are unhappy with them?'

'Unhappy?' She realized he thought she did not like the beautiful things he'd had sent from Rumaillah. 'No! They're lovely, but—'

'They do not fit?' He made a dismissive gesture. 'That is not a problem. They can be changed.'

'No!'

His eyes narrowed, but she refused to be intimidated. 'Just listen to me, will you? I don't know if they fit or not. There's no point in trying them on.' Now he was silent. 'I can't afford such expensive clothes.'

'The cost is immaterial,' he said evenly. 'I do not expect you to pay for them.'

She hadn't for one moment thought that he did. On reflection, even he must have realized that a basic travel policy wouldn't cover designer clothes. But that wasn't the point.

'I can't accept them as a gift.'

'I understand,' he said. 'Of course it would not be appropriate for a married woman to accept clothes from another man. I will send a full account to your husband.'

'Oh, right. I see. Well, take my advice, Han. Don't accept a cheque.'

She struggled to stand, but before she could organize her crutches to make her getaway, Hanif had taken them from her, put them out of reach. Was beside her.

'Why did you marry this man, Lucy?'

She did not move, did not answer. What could she say? That she had been a fool? That she'd craved love and he'd been there when she'd been adrift, alone. A life raft.

A leaky, rotten life raft…

She closed eyes that, without warning, began to sting and, unable to speak, simply shook her head.

'It is clear from everything you say that he has not shown you the respect, the honour, that you deserve,' he said more gently and somehow he was sitting beside her and she had a tissue in her hand. 'Why did you marry him?'

But she refused to break down and cry, instead managing a careless shrug. 'Because he made it so easy.'

'Easy?'

How could she make him understand?

'Gran was so afraid that I'd be like my mother, go off the rails. Maybe I should have fought harder, but by the time I was old enough for meaningful rebellion I'd worked out that my best way of escape would be university.' She looked up at him, hoping that he would understand. She hadn't wimped out. Her major asset had been her brains and she'd used them. 'Then she had the stroke and there was no escape.'

'When she died, you were alone?'

'Alone, completely lost. And suddenly Steve was there, a prop, taking away the need to think. It was just so easy.'

He frowned. 'You knew him?'

She nodded. 'His family lived around the

corner from us. Steve was in the same year as me in school.'

'You had been in love with him since then?'

'In love?' She shrugged. 'There wasn't a girl in the school who wasn't a little in love with Steve Mason. He stood head and shoulders above everyone, you know?' She turned to him, unsure whether he would understand. 'He was a straight A student, great at sports, always wore the latest must-have clothes. He even had a motorbike.'

'Deadly,' he agreed, with the faintest of smiles, and she knew that he was speaking from personal experience. Of course even the oldest, grandest of British public schools took girls at sixth form level these days and she had no doubt that, in the hothouse atmosphere of a boarding school, Hanif would have been a danger to the heart of any girl.

But she raised her eyebrows and somewhat mischievously said, 'The motorbike?'

'What else?' he replied. 'Dangerous things.'

'I'll bet you had one.'

'My father forbade it,' he said. Then, when she lifted her brows a fraction higher, 'But yes, you are right. I had a motorbike. So, where did Steve Mason take you on this dangerous machine?'

'Me?'

'I assumed that there must have been a long-standing arrangement between you. Something of which your grandmother would not have approved.'

'She'd have locked me up in the cellar rather than let me out with Steve Mason,' she assured him. 'With or without the motorbike. But the situation never arose. He never even knew I existed back then.'

'I find that hard to believe.'

'You wouldn't, not if you'd seen me. I wore the most unattractive charity shop clothes my grand-mother could find, my hair scragged back in a plait. Not a scrap of make-up.'

'A woman does not need make-up to be beau-tiful. It is in the bones, in the character, in the heart.'

'You might think that. I might like to believe that. But when you're in the sixth form and the object of desire is an eighteen-year-old boy with a soul as deep as an August puddle, you need make-up. The works. Believe me. Not even the cool girls wanted to be seen with me.'

'Then I do not understand. If you had not been kept apart by your grandmother, how did you meet, marry, so quickly after her death? It is a matter of months, you said.'

'I think the official term is "swept off your feet".'

Actually, it hadn't been so much 'swept' as gently lifted on a tide of yearning to belong. To be like other women. To come in from the cold.

'I hadn't seen him for years, not since I left school. He went off to university, never came home to live after that. Then, when Gran died, I found out that she'd left me the house.' She glanced at him, but it was impossible to tell what he was thinking. 'She'd always told me that she was going to leave it to her church, but at the last minute she relented, or perhaps she was afraid my mother would turn up and challenge the will, demand what was rightfully hers.'

'And then this man appeared, magically, on your doorstep. Prince Charming to your Cinderella.'

'That's almost scary.'

'What is?'

'The Cinderella thing. I was wearing an apron, my hair tied up in a scarf, sweeping the path…'

'Oh.'

'He stopped, looked up at the For Sale sign, then at me, then he said, "Lucy Forrester…"' She gave a little shrug. 'I couldn't believe he remembered my name.'

Han forced himself to get up, walk away, using the excuse of pouring a glass of water for her.

From the outside it was so easy to see what had happened. She had been left property and, alone, with no one to advise her, she had been a gift for a man who had no doubt been using women since he'd been a youth.

Add to that the disappearance of the burned out 4x4, the denial that she'd ever been to the Bouheira Tours office, and it occurred to him that her disappearance might suit her husband extremely well. That she might, in fact, be in very real danger.

There was no way that he could allow Lucy to leave his protection until he'd talked to the man, made it plain that Lucy was under his personal protection. That if anything bad happened to her he would find himself removed from society— not comfortably ensconced in a well-lit cell in a modern prison, but dropped in the darkest oubliette in one of those long-forgotten mountaintop forts that would never make any list of tourist attractions.

He forced his mouth into a smile before turning to Lucy, handing her the glass. 'So, there you were,' he said, 'Prince Charming himself ready to sweep you away on his Harley. What happened next?'

'Nothing dramatic. He said he'd heard about my grandmother. How sorry he was. How tough it was that I'd missed out on university…'

She lifted her hand in an unconscious gesture that said more than the words she couldn't manage about how hard that must have been for her.

She sipped the water, put down the glass and said, 'I asked him, as you do, what he was doing now. He told me that he'd got a job with an offshore bank here in Ramal Hamrah, but had immediately seen the potential for tourism, not just the standard dune-surfing operations that were opening up in other states, but for longer trips out into the desert to oasis camps, to archaeological sites. As soon as he'd managed to scrape together the capital, he set up Bouheira Tours.'

'Zahir is always telling me of the possibilities,' Han said. Then, 'What was he doing looking at houses in the UK if he was so busy building up his business?'

'Property prices were rocketing and he thought he ought to get a foothold in the market. Somewhere he could let while he was away. He wanted it near to his mother so that she could keep an eye on it for him.'

'Did he make an offer? For the house?'

'Well, no. He'd just been looking around the neighbourhood to see what was available. As soon as he said it was a buy-to-let I knew my house was wrong for him. It needs a lot of work and he would want somewhere modern, ready to go. He didn't even come in, but as he turned to go he stopped and asked me if I'd have dinner with him that evening.' She smiled. 'And no, he wasn't riding a Harley, he was driving his mother's old Ford. Far from sweeping me off my feet, Han, it was pretty clear that everyone he knew had moved on and I was the only person saving him from a night in front of the television with his mother.'

'Good dinner?'

'I can't remember. We talked about Ramal Hamrah, mostly. He made it sound magical. Encouraged me to come and visit once I'd sold the house. I didn't actually believe he meant it.'

'Why not?'

'It's just the sort of thing people say, isn't it? I just said it sounded lovely and I'd think about it and then he took me home, thanked me for a lovely evening and drove away. I didn't expect to see him again.'

'How long before he was back?'

'I was on my way upstairs to bed when he phoned, asked me if I'd spend the next day looking at houses with him.' She looked down at her hands as if embarrassed by her gullibility. 'He made it all so easy,' she said again. 'I'd never been on a date, didn't know what a man would expect, but Steve never did anything to make me feel uncomfortable. He was just so different from what I'd expected. From the way he'd been at school.' She looked at him, pulled a face. 'Still as gorgeous, still the kind of man who turned heads in the street, but Prince Charming himself couldn't have been more circumspect.'

'Never trust a man…' he began, then stopped.

'Never trust a man who doesn't want to get into your knickers?' she said, completing the sentence for him and doing it with a smile, more because of his reluctance to embarrass her, than because she found it amusing. 'Because if he doesn't want sex, you have to ask yourself what he does want.'

'I'm sorry. I shouldn't have implied—'

'It's okay, Han. Life is a steep learning curve and I started later than most, but I'm getting there.'

'How long did he wait before he asked you to marry him?'

She really didn't want to talk about it any more, but Han had been patient. He had a right to know what he'd got himself into.

'Not long. He said…'

No. She really, really didn't want to think about the soft, sweet lies Steve had told her and waved her hand as if pushing the words away.

Han caught it and, before she knew how it had happened, her face was in his shoulder, her cheek against the smooth cloth of his robe.

'I shouldn't have asked,' he said. 'It doesn't matter.'

'He was so sweet.' She lifted her head, looked up at him. 'He said I should take the house off the market, that when he came back from Ramal Hamrah we'd do it up together so that I could sell it for what it was really worth.'

'A friend in need.'

'For the first time in my life I thought someone actually cared about me,' she admitted. 'But there was a problem. I had no training, no job, no money. It had taken every bit of Gran's old-age pension and my carer's allowance to keep us alive and now she was dead I had no income of any kind.'

She didn't bother to mention the much larger private pension that her grandfather had provided, that could have made their life so much easier. She hadn't known about that until afterwards, when she had to sort out her grandmother's papers, and had discovered that it had been paid direct to the church each month.

'The house was my only asset. I was nearly twenty-eight years old and had never worked; the only jobs open to me paid the minimum wage. There was no way I could afford even the most basic running costs. That's when Steve said we should get married right away. So that he could take care of me.'

'That's when he swept you off your feet.'

'He brought all these forms from banks, credit card companies, changing the address on them to mine, adding my name to his accounts, not even waiting until we were married.'

She couldn't look at him, but he cradled her cheek and gently turned her face so that she had no choice.

'He borrowed money on them?'

'Oh, yes…' her laughter was mirthless '…and don't those banks love to lend money?'

'And the cards, of course, were not his, but new ones he'd applied for in your name.'

'You see? You got it straight away. Why was I so dumb?'

'Because it never occurred to you that he would do anything so wicked.'

'Pretty naïve, in retrospect. I mean this was Steve Mason. Why would he look at me twice?'

'I've had a new mirror fitted in the bathroom, Lucy. Maybe you should take a look in it.'

'Oh, *please.*' Then, because she didn't want

him to think she was totally stupid, she said, 'I did actually read all the forms he brought me to sign. Even the small print. They were all what he said they were. I guess it must have been the ones underneath, the ones he said were copies and just lifted the top copy for me to sign in duplicate, that he sent to the banks.'

'I imagine that if he'd worked in a bank he must have known all the ways to work a fraud. Is that it?'

She wished.

'He made me a partner in Bouheira Tours as a wedding present. I imagine the papers that I signed, in quadruplicate, are fakes. At least some of them. Somewhere in amongst them was the big one. The guarantee for a loan against the house.'

'I'm not surprised you were in such a break-neck speed to catch up with him.'

'Yes,' she said. Then, not quite meeting his eyes, 'I think it's just as well I rolled the 4x4. At least this way I'm not languishing in a Ramal Hamrah jail on a charge of grievous bodily harm or worse.'

'You would not have hurt him,' Han began, but hesitated and she knew he was wondering if

Steve would have hurt her. 'But you might easily have killed yourself.'

'I know. What I did was stupid. I just wanted…' She stopped. 'It doesn't matter. All I have to do is sell the house, pay my debts and learn my lesson.'

'All?'

'Yes, Han. That's all. Since I never expected to inherit it, I'm exactly where I expected to be when my grandmother died. The pity of it is that she changed her mind about leaving the house to the church. That way she'd have saved everyone a great deal of trouble.'

CHAPTER SEVEN

HAN could not believe Lucy was going to allow this man to get away with stealing from her.

She was shivering just from the memory and he held her closer, wanting to warm her with his own heat. He'd told Zahir that having saved her life he was responsible for her but they both knew that he could have done everything that needed to be done from a distance.

It went deeper than duty, deeper than the care of a stranger in need. From the moment he'd set eyes on her, it had always been more personal than that.

He'd saved her life and now he wanted to save…her life.

'You really need to take legal advice before you do anything, Lucy,' he said, keeping it as businesslike as it could be with his arms around her.

'Good money after bad,' she said. 'There's nothing anyone can do.'

'There is always something.' But he was speaking to himself rather than her.

'I talked to the card companies, explained what had happened. They produced the forms I'd signed and what could I say? They had paid up in good faith. They didn't do anything wrong, Han. It was my responsibility to read what I was signing.'

'You trusted him. He took advantage of that. And what about the mortgage? You knew nothing about that. He tricked you into signing the papers. I'm no lawyer, but that sounds like a clear case of fraud to me.'

'They explained it very clearly. It's my house and he is…'

'Your husband,' he said, filling the gap when she faltered. He had to remind himself of that. Keep reminding himself.

'That was why he married me.' She shuddered.

'You make your mistakes, Han, and you have to pay for them.'

He knew that was true. And that some debts could not be paid with money…

As if suddenly aware just how close they were, how tightly he was holding her, Lucy eased herself away from him, out of his arms.

'I'm sorry,' she said carefully. 'I didn't intend to burden you with my problems.' Her smile did a good job of masking everything she must be feeling—the rage, utter helplessness in the face of such treachery. 'You shouldn't have been so stubborn about sending back the clothes. If you'd agreed with me, you wouldn't have been forced to listen to me wittering on like this.'

It was harder than it should have been to let her go, but then he shouldn't have been holding her in the first place.

'I'll remember for next time,' he assured her. He'd remember that disregarding her wishes brought her close, opened her up. Encouraged her to talk.

'Then you will send them back?'

'If you insist,' he said, standing up, a hand ready to help her to her feet if she needed it, but she used the arm of the sofa to lever herself up. 'I must, of course, do as you ask.'

'Thank you.'

He handed her the crutches, let her reach the

door before he said, 'There is just one small problem.'

She didn't turn around, didn't ask him what the small problem was, but waited for him to tell her; he could tell from the way she kept her eyes facing forward, lifted her a head a little, that she knew she wasn't going to like it, whatever it was.

She was probably right, but there was no way in this world that he was going to ask Zahir's sister, or his own for that matter, to return the clothes they'd bought and replace them with chain store versions.

'If I return these clothes what are you going to wear?'

That got her.

'I…' She glanced back over her shoulder and, as her eyes met his, she thought better of whatever she'd been about to say. 'If you could replace them with something more in line with my financial situation, I would be most grateful. Just a few things to keep me going until I can get home.'

Back to the charity shops, no doubt.

'Of course. I understand. That will mean a delay, of course. I will have to find someone who is prepared to undertake such a task. While Zahir's sister was happy to spend time choosing clothes for you from her favourite designers, she would, I think, baulk at visiting the *souk.*'

'I'm not totally helpless,' she said. 'Take me to Rumaillah and I'll do it myself.'

'Of course. Whatever you wish.' He waited until he saw the tension drain from her shoulders, then said, 'But first you will need something to wear.' He let his gaze travel the length of her body before meeting her gaze head on. 'Unless, of course, it is your intention to cause a riot in the streets?'

Her mouth opened, but nothing emerged and after a moment or two she closed it again.

'It will mean waiting another day, maybe two,' he continued, since she appeared to have lost the power of speech, or perhaps had chosen discretion over candour. 'And of course another trip for the helicopter. Will your insurance company pay for that, do you think? Will you ask them?' Not waiting for her to reply—the question was outrageous, unworthy—he went on, 'While we are waiting, you're going to need to borrow some basics to tide you over.'

Her eyes remained fixed on his, defiant to the

last, but her shoulders had slumped in defeat and it was difficult to keep up the act. But if that was what it took to make her accept the clothes, that was what he would have to do.

'You will find a walk-in closet off your room,' he continued, with a dismissive gesture that under normal circumstances came as naturally to him as breathing. These were not normal circumstances and he had to force himself to treat the matter as if it was of no consequence. 'Noor was not as tall as you, nor as slender, but I'm sure you'll find something you can wear. Take what you need.'

'You don't mean that.' She gave up on looking over her shoulder and, carefully balancing herself on her crutches, she turned around so that she was confronting him head on. 'You're just making a point, aren't you?'

Of course he was. He knew she would not wear Noor's clothes, not because she had a problem with used clothes—she'd already told him that she'd been dressed in charity shop donations all her life—but because she believed it would distress him.

He wasn't about to disabuse her of that idea.

'And if I am,' he replied, 'are you getting it?'

'The point being,' she said slowly, 'that you have gone out of your way to provide me with everything I need. That I'm being a pain in the backside. That I should quit while I'm ahead.'

'You appear to have mastered the essentials.' Then, because he could not resist it, 'Of course I would not have been so ungallant as to comment on your backside, no matter how painful.'

'I believe the colloquialism refers to your backside rather than mine,' she said, scowling, he suspected, to prevent herself from laughing.

'I stand corrected. English is such a complex language; I fear the finer points occasionally escape me.'

That did it. 'You are so full of it, Han,' she said, finally breaking down and letting a bubble of laughter escape. 'I don't appear to have much choice, do I?'

'There is always a choice, Lucy, but believe me when I tell you that the simple pleasure you gave two young women today,' he said, magnanimous in victory, 'and the goodwill I have accrued by providing my sister with enough speculative gossip to keep the females in my family entertained for weeks, far outweighs the small cost involved.'

'Gossip? You mean...' She clearly did not want to voice what she thought he meant and instead said, '*Your* sister? I thought it was Zahir's sister who had drawn the short straw. Or would that be the long one?'

'For the pleasure of spending money without having to account for it to their husbands? What do you think?'

'I think I'd better say thank you and shut up before you award me some Ramal Hamrah decoration for services to entertainment.'

Beaten, struggling between laughter and rage, Lucy retreated to her sitting room and sat amongst the piles of bags and boxes, touching fabrics she'd only thought of wearing in her wildest teenage dreams. Wallowing guiltily in the luxury of it all, she discovered that it was tears that threatened to overwhelm her as she touched the softest silk to her cheek.

'Lucy...'

Ameerah's voice jerked her back to the present. The child was standing in the doorway, her expression anxious.

'Hello, sweetheart,' she said, sniffing back the

threatening tears, smiling as she reached out a hand, inviting her to come and play. 'Do you want to help me unpack?'

She needed no further encouragement and together they dived into the boxes, spreading clothes over every surface. They exclaimed over the colours, sprayed scent on each other, laughed, talked—the words didn't matter. Two females exclaiming over clothes were always going to be talking the same language.

'What shall I wear?' Lucy finally asked, her gestures, making the meaning clear. Then, 'What would *you* wear?'

Ameerah went straight for a raw silk *shalwar kameez* in a deep glowing red, holding the top up against her small body.

'Good choice!' she exclaimed, clapping. The outfit was stunning, sophisticated, exotic. She might be only three years old, but this little girl clearly knew what she wanted, what was due to her. 'Well, that's you sorted,' she said, helping the child into it, laughing as she paraded with all the haughty air of a catwalk model. Then she looked around a little desperately for something ordinary that she would feel at home in. Everything was so beautiful. So stylish.

Nothing was *her.*

But she had to wear something and, in the absence of anything as plain as a white cotton shirt, she chose the nearest alternative in amber silk, teaming it with a pair of beautifully cut black linen trousers that amongst the jewel-bright colours were positively understated.

Unfortunately, the legs of the trousers proved too narrow to accommodate the splint. Ameerah, who had not been impressed with the trousers, offered her a rich blue kaftan as an alternative.

The style was practical, but Lucy picked out one in silvery grey, with black embroidery around the hem, at the wrists, the neck. It was not exactly plain, but it was more in keeping with her Anglo-Saxon need to blend into the surroundings.

Ameerah pulled a face but accepted her decision and set about finding a scarf to go with it while Lucy confronted the piles of sexy underwear.

For a girl, woman, who'd never worn anything but plain white and practical, the underwear was a revelation, but since it quickly became clear that every outfit had been teamed with its own matching bra and pants, choice was not a problem. Grey silk it was.

Han was right. Those two women had really enjoyed themselves at his expense.

Lucy, anxious now to shower and get into some real clothes, sent Ameerah to show herself to Fathia, then braced herself to face her reflection in the bathroom mirror.

The bruising was shocking, it was true, but her eye was open now and the swelling was nowhere near as bad as she'd imagined.

She unfastened her hair and, for just a moment, held the thin leather cord that Han had used to tie it back, touched it to her cheek as she had the silk. Then, about to place it on top of the nightdress and robe that had once belonged to his wife, knowing that as soon as she left the room someone would come and clear them away, she tucked it into the pocket of the bathrobe.

She managed the shower more easily this time, even washed her hair without too much difficulty. She was recovering, she thought. Regaining her strength. Regaining her life. She was even getting about on her crutches without help. In a day or two she'd be able to leave Rawdah al-'Arusah, return to the real world.

And tried to feel a little happier about that.

She'd half expected to find Ameerah waiting for her when she emerged in her new bathrobe, her hair wrapped in a towel, but the sitting room was empty, although someone had folded the clothes, had brought them through to the bedroom and taken away all the empty packaging.

The toiletries had been neatly arranged on the dressing table, along with combs, brushes, hairpins. There was a hair-dryer, too. Not a new one, though.

She didn't bother with make-up; there was, after all, nothing that could cover up the interesting colour effects. She just dried her hair, trying not to think about the way Han had done it for her. Then, rejecting the pull of the leather cord in her pocket, she pinned it at the nape with the intricate silver clip.

When she was done, she slipped her feet into a pair of grey ballet-style pumps made from butter-soft suede, picked up the long palest primrose scarf that Ameerah had selected for her and stepped out onto the balcony to cool herself in the breeze from the mountains.

Han saw Lucy long before she saw him.

Jamilla, his youngest sister, had called him from Rumaillah, wanting details of Lucy's colouring. Zahir, she'd said, had been no use whatever. On reflection, he wondered if that was true or whether Milly had made an excuse to find out if he'd noticed the colour of his guest's eyes.

Whatever her reason, he had to admit that she'd chosen well. The light grey silk, caught by the breeze, moulded itself to Lucy's figure. With a pale scarf draped loosely over her hair and floating over her shoulders to the ground, she looked more like a fairy tale princess from a tale woven by Scheherazade than some modern western woman with the troubles of the world on her shoulders.

Then, as if suddenly aware that she was not alone, she turned, saw him, smiled, and something deep inside him warmed and smiled back.

'You look stronger, Lucy Forrester.'

'I feel stronger. There's something about

wearing nightclothes in the day that makes one feel like an invalid. Just getting dressed has made me feel better,' she said, and then she turned away quickly, but not before he saw that her cheeks burned.

'You must not do too much too quickly,' he said, and he burned too, thinking, as she must have, that she was dressed, as a wife or mistress would be, wrapped at his insistence, in clothes it pleased him to see her wear. Knew that every time the breeze caught the silk, brushed it against her skin, she would remember that.

For a woman to wear the clothes that a man had bought her was to feel his touch with every movement. For a man to hear the whisper of cloth as she walked, was to feel her response to him, the throb of her pulse as it intensified, the silky heat between her thighs as she waited for him to unwrap her.

It hadn't occurred to him that she would feel this. She had not been brought up to think in that way, not taught that her role was to please her husband. But neither was she like the western women he had met in his youth, at university, in the free and easy days before he'd buckled down to duty, accepted the bride his family had chosen for him. Spirited women who took life head-on, denied themselves nothing, knew everything, or thought they did.

He had enjoyed their company, had taken pleasure in their freedom, admired their directness. Lucy had something of their spirit in her character, but she had an innocence too, like a girl before she had been touched by a man. Knowing but unknowing. Afraid and yet trembling with eagerness.

And he was clearly losing his mind.

'I was wondering, Han, would it be acceptable for me to write notes to your sister, to Zahir's sister, to thank them for taking such trouble on my behalf today? I accept your assurance that they enjoyed themselves, but even so.'

'I know that Jamilla would be touched by the thought.'

'Thank you. And I'd like to see more of the garden before I leave,' she said, as the silence between them stretched to breaking point. 'If I may? Are there places where I should not go?'

'You are free to wander where you will, Lucy. No one will bother you.'

'I was thinking that I might be the one causing a disturbance. You said there is a hunting lodge. I'd hate to blunder into some men-only territory, make anyone uncomfortable.'

She had the courage to hunt down a fraudster in his own territory, yet she retained the air of a virgin, had all the instincts of a princess. She would grace the garden with her presence.

'You need not concern yourself,' he said.

His men, those who came to hunt, those who worked here, would melt away at her approach. She would never suspect they were there unless she needed help and, unless it was urgent, they would summon him to provide it.

She was under his protection and they would treat her with the same respect as they would any woman in his family. The same respect they would show towards his wife.

About to offer to show her the hidden beauties of the garden, he instead inclined his head and said, 'The garden is yours, *sitti.*'

Sitti? It was a word Lucy was unfamiliar with and she wished she had her language CDs, her phrase book. Already her ear was becoming accustomed to the sounds and this would have been the perfect place to continue with her studies of the language.

Sitti. My lady...

Han stepped back within the safety of his study, crossed to his desk, hunted desperately amongst the drawers for the photograph of Noor that he had put away, unable to bear the love in her eyes.

He set it where it belonged, where he would see it every time he looked up. Touched her face with his fingers as he had done a thousand times before, as if he could somehow call her back, as he'd tried to hold her in this world when all she wanted to do was leave it.

'I did everything I could to keep her alive,' he said, aware that Lucy had followed him, was standing in the doorway. He didn't turn. Already she was filling the places in his home, in his head, that belonged to Noor.

If he turned from the photograph to look at Lucy, the image, already fading, would become fainter. Her voice, her laughter, dimmed to nothing more than a distant rustle in the memory.

'She wanted to come back here, spend some time with her baby. Die in peace,' he said, jabbing himself with the words. 'I couldn't let her go, wouldn't let her go, and to please me she spent the end of her days in the hospital, having the treatment that was too late to do anything but cause her pain.'

Lucy propped her crutches against his desk, took the photograph from him, looked at it for a while.

'She was very beautiful.'

'It was Noor who broke the mirror,' he said. 'In the bathroom. She threw a bottle of scent at her reflection, unable to bear what was happening to her. She thought she had become ugly.'

'How could she have believed herself ugly when she only had to see herself reflected in your eyes to know how you loved her?'

He frowned, looking at Lucy, not the photograph she was holding out to him.

'I've seen the way your eyes soften as you speak of her, Han. Appearances may alter, but love is constant.'

'Is it? If I'd loved her, I'd have let her die as she wished—at home, with her baby in her arms.' He'd never voiced his guilt before, had never said the words out loud. He'd kept them locked up inside him, afraid that if the pain of it escaped it would devour him. He didn't know why he was doing it now. Only that since Lucy's accident everything inside him felt shaken up, disturbed. Like a numb limb coming back to painful life. He looked at her now, as if it was her fault, and demanded, 'How can I forgive myself for that?'

'You're human, Han. You couldn't bear to lose her. She knew that.'

'Being human is an excuse?'

'It's why she broke the mirror. Her reflection was a constant reminder to her that she was never going to see her baby grow into a young woman, have children of her own. That she wasn't going to grow old with you in this garden.'

Lucy had followed him on pure instinct. Nothing in his expression, his voice, had indicated that she had said or done anything to offend him, yet the abruptness with which he'd left her was so at odds with his usual manner that she had barely been able to stop herself from reaching out to him, holding him beside her.

She'd left it a few moments, telling herself that she was wrong, giving herself time to think.

But it had been no good. Something had disturbed him. While self-preservation had suggested it would be wiser to take advantage of his invitation to make free with his garden and leave him to get over it, she had found she could not simply walk away.

She'd had the excuse of asking him for paper, a pen, to write her thank you letters while the moment was fresh, should she need it.

Too late she wished she had chosen the garden option, not because she didn't have the answer to his question, but because she did. From the outside, looking in, it was easy to see that he was angry with Noor, angry with Ameerah, and he hated himself for it.

Easy to tell him that he would not find self-forgiveness in a photograph, that he must look to the living, to his daughter, for that. To tell him that only when he'd forgiven her for living when Noor was dead, to find it in his heart to love her as a father should, would he be able to forgive himself.

Move on.

Easy, but impossible. Besides, she was certain that at some untapped, deeper level of consciousness he already knew it. If it was that easy, he would have done it long ago.

All she could do, would do, in the limited time available to her, was to make herself a bridge between them. Hope that he could find the way across.

'You loved her, Han.' She set the photograph carefully on the desk. 'She submitted to the treatment because she loved you, wanted you to be able to feel that you had done everything possible.'

'How do you know that?'

'Because it is what I would have done,' she said truthfully. 'She did it because she chose to, not because you insisted.'

He stared at her.

'You could not make her hurt her child, Han. Do you truly believe that she would have let you hurt her?'

She might be so far out on a limb here that she was about to drop off the end, but she could only say what she believed. And she believed—no, she knew—that Noor would have been willing to suffer anything to save Han from what must have been desperate feelings of helplessness.

She gave a little shake of her head.

There was no point in telling him that the last thing his wife would have wanted was for him to spend the rest of his life beating himself up with guilt. He was right, he should have accepted Noor's decision, but desperation made fools of us all, and maybe Noor, human and afraid, had hoped a little too, that somehow, against all the odds, he might in the end save her.

Instead she briefly rested her hand on his sleeve, an instinctive gesture of reassurance, then lowering her head in the slightest of bows, she said, 'I'm sorry. I have disturbed you.'

As she turned away Han half reached for her, then, as if burned, he snatched his hand back, let it drop. 'What did you want, Lucy?'

'Nothing. It does not matter.' Then, 'Just some notepaper. And a pen.'

'You were brought up to write your thank you letters before you enjoyed your gifts?'

He was, she thought, mocking her. In truth, thank you letters hadn't featured much in her childhood, but she smiled and said, 'It's just good manners.'

He took notepaper and envelopes from a stand on his desk, found a pen. Handed them to her.

'And their names? Jamilla al-Khatib?'

She spelled it out and he nodded, clearly impatient for her to be gone. 'I'll have to ask her which of Zahir's sisters accompanied her.'

Han watched her swing easily away from him on her crutches, her name already filling his mouth, to call her back, before he caught himself, tightening his hand into a fist, rubbing it against the place on his sleeve where she had touched him as if to capture her essence, to hold it fast.

Her own life was in turmoil and yet she'd brought him a glimpse of peace, as if she had opened the door a crack and shown him a way through to warmth and light.

He took a step after her, pulled himself up, confused, turning to snatch up the telephone as if it was an anchor holding him in place, punched the button on the fast dial.

'Hanif. How good to hear your voice.'

Milly's voice was warm, but he caught the subtext. That it had been too long since he'd called her.

'I wanted to thank you for your time today. I realise how onerous a task it must have been.'

She tutted at his sarcasm. 'Did your guest have everything she needs?'

'Everything and more, I suspect.'

'She may have needs she is too shy to mention to a man who is not her husband.'

If her husband was any kind of a man, he thought, it wouldn't be necessary.

He said, 'I doubt it.'

Lucy might blush like a maiden, but she didn't seem to have any problems communicating with him. On the contrary, the insight she'd given him into Noor's state of mind in those last weeks had been like hearing her speak from the grave.

A superstitious man might have believed her to be a *Peri,* one of those fair spirits, endowed with grace and beauty, who inhabited the empty places, a genie, sent to guide him from the wilderness.

'Hanif?'

'I'm sure you covered every possibility. She will be writing to thank you herself. In fact that was my reason for calling you; I need the name of your partner in retail therapy.'

She laughed. 'It was Dira. I'm so glad she called me. We had a wonderful time.'

'Will you please find her some suitable gift? A token, from the family, of our appreciation for her help.'

'Of course.'

'And when Lucy's fit enough to come down to Rumaillah to sort out her passport, can you find time to take her to stores where she can buy the sort of clothes she would normally wear in England? Nothing too expensive. She can't afford designer labels and she'll insist on paying for it herself.'

'An independent woman.'

'Yes,' he agreed. But not independent enough for the totally inappropriate responses she stirred in him.

He needed to distance himself a little from Lucy.

Distance himself a lot.

With that in mind, he put through a call to Fathia, suggesting she ask Lucy to spend the evening with her, to eat with her, then he wrote Dira's name on a sheet of paper, planning to leave it for her before he took himself to the lodge to eat with men whose conversation would consist of nothing more disturbing than the speed of their horses, the superiority of their falcons, the stamina of their camels.

Lucy's room, however, was empty. No doubt she was taking advantage of the cool evening air to enjoy the garden. Which was good.

He crossed to the table to leave the note, saw the book of poems he'd given her lying open. Unable to help himself, he picked it up to see what had caught her attention—

'…In the Garden of Paradise vainly thou'lt seek
The lip of the fountain of Roknabad
And the bowers of Musalla where roses twine…'

As he snapped it shut a piece of paper, folded in two, flew out from between the pages and fell to the floor. He'd had no intention of looking at it, but as he picked it up it fell open and he found himself looking at a childish drawing of three people.

A family. A father, a mother and a child.

The detail was minimal but even so there was no mistaking who they were meant to represent.

And when he looked up Lucy was in the doorway, hand in hand with the traitorous little artist.

While he had been struggling with feelings that threatened to overwhelm him, threatened to obliterate Noor from his memory, his life, her precious daughter had abandoned her without thought for the more immediate gratification of having someone with arms to hug her.

Someone living, breathing, with a heart that could love her back.

CHAPTER EIGHT

'HAN…'

Lucy flinched as he crushed the paper in his hand and flung it into the corner, putting her arm protectively around Ameerah as she turned to hide herself in the folds of her dress.

'Han, it doesn't mean anything,' she protested. 'She's a little girl. She doesn't understand.'

'But you do. You sat and watched her, encouraged her…' He stormed towards the door, but she stood her ground. 'Let me pass, Lucy.'

'Where are you going?' she demanded. Demanded! She had no right to ask him what time of day it was…

'Nowhere. To the desert. A place as empty as I am. A place where the air smells of nothing. Where each day the sand is wiped clean. Where there are no memories.'

Then, somehow he was by her, striding away

down the wide corridor, the fine camel-hair cloak thrown over his shoulders flying behind him, shining like gold in the light. It hadn't been a hallucination, she thought.

He was her angel…

'It isn't true,' she called after him. 'You carry your memories with you.' He made no indication that he'd heard. 'Good and bad. They become part of you, make you what you are.' She lifted her voice, insisting on being heard. 'You have to live with them, Han. You have to live…'

But he was gone.

She sighed, wishing she could have made him listen, but he was hurting and, however unintentionally, she was the cause of his pain.

She knelt beside Ameerah, holding her close. 'It'll be all right, sweetheart,' she said softly. 'He doesn't mean it. Your daddy loves you; he just can't allow himself to feel anything right now because it hurts too much. One day he'll come and take your hand. He'll pick you up, hug you so hard you'll think you might die of happiness.'

And she kept on saying it until she wasn't sure whether it was Ameerah or the desperate, motherless little girl she had once been she was talking to.

Hanif did not return for days.

As the reality of what that meant gradually sank in, she looked at the beauty, the luxury around her in a different way. It had seemed like a refuge, but now… Well, she was the one who'd suggested this was a harem and, despite Han's suggestion that it was a place of power, she caught a closer glimpse of the truth. He wasn't keeping her against her will, but without him to authorise it no one seemed capable of doing anything to get her home.

Short of embarrassing the British Ambassador—and she had enough problems without appealing to the Foreign Office to extricate her from the home of the Emir's youngest son—she was stuck at al-'Arusah for the foreseeable future. And when she asked Fathia—the only other person around who spoke any English—when he was likely to return, her only response was a shrug and, *'Bukra, insha'Allah.'*

Tomorrow. If God wills.

She suspected she should have been more agitated, upset, even angrier than she was, but actually it seemed pointless, a waste of energy. He would return. She would go home.

In the meantime she'd done everything possible to sort out her finances. Had instructed the solicitor who'd handled her grandmother's affairs to begin procedures to extricate her with the utmost speed from her marriage.

All she could do now was search for a job so that she could take her own advice and 'live' and, aware that she was unlikely to impress prospective employers with her black eyes and crutches, she did what Hanif had insisted she do—before he'd lost his temper and stormed out.

She relaxed, spent time exploring both the pavilion and the garden. Helped herself to the books in Hanif's library.

Oh, and she wrote to Jamilla and Dira.

Jamilla phoned her, encouraging her to ask for anything else she needed and inviting her to come and stay when she returned to Rumaillah. She'd been so chatty, informal, charming that Lucy had been bold enough to ask not only for a replacement for her lost Arabic language CD, but for books, toys, anything likely to amuse Ameerah, keep her occupied.

She hadn't anticipated the difference between her vision of what a three-year-old needed and what a Ramal Hamrah princess might consider appropriate for a tiny princess in waiting.

It wasn't all bad.

The tricycle, for instance, was a huge hit. The books and jigsaw puzzles filled quiet afternoons, although Ameerah ignored the brightly coloured crayons, clinging instead to the pastels Hanif had provided for her artwork.

The pair of Siamese kittens were, perhaps, a gift too far for a rather wild three-year-old, but Lucy was enchanted with the way they curled up together by her feet as she practised her Arabic, followed her as she walked in the garden with Fathia, listening to her stories about Han. How wild he'd been as a boy. How fearless.

How like him Ameerah was.

She suffered the most painful lurch of her stomach when she heard how he'd nearly killed himself playing polo. Felt a disturbing mixture of sympathy and relief when assured that he'd given up the sport for his mother's sake, turned to more serious things, taking on the role of diplomat to please his father.

Learned how this man who'd touched her so deeply, had been the adored youngest son, a golden boy who could do no wrong and had, in a few short years of manhood, become a credit to his family and his country.

Which, Lucy thought, explained a lot. When you lived your life in the sun, perfect in every way, it must be cold in the shadows. Impossible to forgive yourself the smallest of mistakes.

They were sitting in the summer house, keeping an eye on Ameerah, who was chasing butterflies around the pool.

Lucy, who suspected that she was supposed to join in the breast-beating at the harshness of fate, at Hanif's grief, thought there was more than enough of that to go around, but was saved from saying so by the predictable becoming reality.

'Ameerah!'

Too late. As the child's attention was caught by the shimmer of a dragonfly, she swivelled on one toe and, as she made a wild lunge towards it, lost her balance and toppled dramatically into the water lilies.

Before Fathia could move, Lucy had waded in,

caught hold of the billowing silk of her dress and hauled her out of the water.

'Brat!' she said. 'You did that on purpose.' Then, 'Look at your gorgeous dress! If you're going to behave like a boy you should be wearing shorts and a T-shirt.'

Ameerah, while not understanding every word, certainly got the meaning, just giggled, wriggled free and turned, planning to wade further in.

Lucy, who'd acted without thinking, was standing up to her thighs in water and realised, too late, that she'd run without a thought for her ankle, that she had nothing to hold on to, that both her feet were sinking into the slippery mud at the bottom of the pond.

Everything that followed seemed to happen in slow motion, as if to someone else. She saw herself open her mouth, cry out as the pain caught up with her. Saw herself crumple as her ankle gave way, the soft billow of rich blue silk swelling around her as she sank into the water.

Then suddenly it was all too real and very loud.

The pain, the cold water, the mud. Only the

shrieking wasn't coming from her but from Ameerah, who'd flung her arms around her neck and, no longer laughing, was instead crying, 'Sorry, sorry, sorry…'

'Hush, it's all right,' she said, turning to Fathia to rescue them both, but it was Hanif wading through the water towards her. Hanif in dark and dusty clothes, a *keffiyeh* wound around his head as if he'd come straight from the stables to find her…

Breathe, she reminded herself. Breathe…

She knew the theory, the in-out, in-out basics of staying alive, but somehow the mechanics of it were beyond her and for a moment she thought she might faint.

'Don't move,' he said, catching her around the shoulders, hunkering down to steady her, but this time his voice was gentle. This time she was not afraid. 'Don't even think about trying to move.'

'No,' she finally managed. 'I'm not going anywhere.'

And for a second it seemed the world stood still.

Then Fathia's anxious voice shattered the silence and Lucy, suspecting that she'd been calling for some time, said, 'If you could just take Ameerah?'

It seemed for ever before he straightened, a lifetime before he bent and took the child from her, holding her, dripping, at arm's length.

No! Not like that! Lucy thought fiercely. *Hold her close to you. Hold her against your heart...*

As if he heard her, he slowly drew the child to him, tucking her against his shoulder. Then, with his arm protectively around her, he waded to the edge of pool.

Fathia said something to him, reached out to take her.

It seemed for ever before he surrendered her. Lucy heard him murmur something, whether to the woman or child she had no way of knowing.

She released a long slow breath as he turned back to her and thought *Yes!* but all she said was, 'Rescuing me is getting to be a full-time occupation.'

'Am I complaining?' Before she could reply, he bent, scooped her up as easily as he'd picked up Ameerah and said, 'This is nothing.'

'Believe me,' she said, trying to ignore the closeness, the fact that the silk of her dress had soaked up the water and that it was now clinging tightly to every curve, 'the alternative, crawling back to the side of the pool on my knees, would not be nothing.'

'But you could have done it. Rescuing me is another matter. A miracle...'

Was he talking about Ameerah? About the fact that he'd held her the way a father should?

Then, realising that he was carrying her into the summer house, 'Han! No, I'm soaking! The mud... The carpets...'

Ignoring her protestations, he laid her on the sofa, propping her up with pillows at her back before kneeling beside her to unfasten and discard the ankle splint and its soggy lining. Then, having eased off her ruined sandals, he unwound his *keffiyeh* and carefully wiped the worst of the mud from her feet, her ankles, before tossing that too aside.

Only then did he sit back on his haunches, look at her and, on the point of scolding him for ruining the cushions, she held her tongue. Without the sun at his back, she could see how gaunt and hollow-eyed he looked, as if he hadn't slept or eaten in days.

Her fault, she thought, her fault and, without thinking, she reached out, wanting to comfort him, tell him how sorry she was, as he would have comforted her. For everything.

He caught her wrist before she could touch his face, held it in a grip of steel.

For what seemed like a year he held her there, an inch away from him. It was not enough. Heat fried the air between them, sucked Lucy's breath from her body, licked along her limbs, reducing to ash all the hellfire lectures she'd been read about what happened to girls who succumbed to their wanton desires.

There was no defence against the power of such feelings, no barrier made that was strong enough to withstand this yearning to be held, kissed, possessed.

She hadn't understood, until this moment, what all the fuss was about.

She felt her mouth soften, her lips part, as his hand loosened its grip on her wrist, slid along the length of her arm until his fingers reached her hair, pulled loose the pin that held it back from her face, slid his hand beneath her hair to hold her, his willing prisoner.

The moment stretched endlessly as he lowered his mouth to hers. Then, as he brushed his lips against hers, she felt something deep inside her dissolve, melt.

All pain was forgotten as he leaned into the kiss, deepening it as a thirsty man might drink at a well and Lucy, blown away, matched his need with a passion, a desperate need, beyond her wildest imaginings and she rose to meet him, wanting to feel the heat, the strength of his body against hers.

As if he knew, felt it too, he caught her at the waist, lifting her, holding her to him as if she were the last woman on earth, while his mouth—hard, almost desperate—obliterated everything but the sensory seduction of his body—the silky sweep of his hair against her cheek, the touch of his fingers at her nape, the salty, dusty taste of his skin.

And finally she understood the force that drove men and women to cross continents, conquer nations, give up their lives.

It ended.

It had to end; the fervour of it was too intense, too powerful to be sustained.

He eased back, broke contact despite the fact that her mouth refused to let go, shamelessly caught at his lower lip, reaching out with her tongue, greedy for more of him.

Eyes closed, he rested his forehead against hers, said, 'You were right, Lucy.'

'R-right?'

'We cannot pick and choose from our memories. Cannot erase them like files from a computer, no matter how profoundly we wish it. They make us what we are.'

It took a moment for his words to sink in. Memories could not be erased. And then, as if someone had turned on a light in her brain, she understood what he'd meant by 'rescue'. He'd turned to her in desperation, hoping that, by some miracle, she could overwrite the memory of his dead wife with her mouth, her body. Drive her from his head.

Rescue him…

The pain that swept through her was a revelation. Until that moment she hadn't realised just how much she felt for this tortured man. How could she have known? She knew nothing of love, of tenderness, of passion.

Steve had romanced her but she'd had no yardstick by which to measure him as a man. She'd mistaken his easy charm for genuine feeling, had mistaken her gratitude, relief at having someone take responsibility for her future, for love.

In one touch, one brief moment of conflagration, she had learned the difference.

This might not be love—how could she know?—but these raw emotions were real enough. She knew that because they touched her, hurt her in a way that her ankle never could. That Steve never could. He'd stolen money from her, but that was nothing. He hadn't changed her life in any way that mattered.

Hanif al-Khatib had stolen her heart and, whatever happened, nothing for her would ever be the same.

Except, of course, she had to act as if the world hadn't just exploded in a rainbow of bright colours. As if the scent of the roses, the cypress trees wasn't suddenly richer, more intense. As if her skin didn't sing with his touch.

She had to pretend it was exactly the same.

'M-memories…' She struggled to speak, had to speak. 'Memories make us what we are, Han.' She did a reasonable job of keeping her voice steady. Not perfect, but under the circumstances, not bad. 'We cannot escape our past. All we can do is use our experience to make a better future.' And, summoning up every fibre of willpower, all the hard-learned self-restraint of her upbringing, she pressed her lips against his forehead, letting them linger a second more than she should have, before, with her hands on his shoulders, she gently pushed him away.

For a moment he continued to hold her, look at her. Then, as if suddenly aware of what he was doing, what he had done, he pulled back, stood up, walked away from her, keeping his back to her until he had himself under control.

When he turned his face was once again expressionless. 'I'm sorry…' he began, stopped. 'I cannot find the words; there are no words—'

'Please…don't. I understand.'

She understood that he was apologising for kissing her. Could not decide whether it made things better or worse.

No.

She knew.

Worse. Infinitely worse.

'I will, of course, make immediate arrangements to have you moved to the protection of my mother's—'

'No! Thank you, Han.'

Oh, right. That made sense. Now he was back and ready to do as she'd asked, to send her to Rumaillah so that she could sort out her documents, leave Ramal Hamrah, leave him in peace, she was resisting it.

She would go. Of course she would. She had no choice. But not like this.

Not with Hanif feeling yet more guilt for having kissed her. Besides, if she left, she had no doubt that he'd use the excuse to send his daughter away too, which was the last thing she wanted.

He'd held her, made a start. He mustn't be allowed to step back now.

'I don't need protection from you,' she said. He neither confirmed nor denied it and, emboldened, she said, 'And I'd rather stay here, where it's cooler, until Zahir has sorted out my papers.' Lying back like a princess against silk pillows, it seemed perfectly natural to make the kind of imperious gesture she'd seen him use a dozen times. 'He is sorting them out, isn't he?'

Han considered mentioning that his family had installed air conditioning some time ago, but discovered a hitherto unsuspected selfish streak in his nature.

Here the air was warm, sultry, laden with the scent of roses. In another world, he would lie here with this woman, they would end what they had begun, make love by moonlight, read poetry, share food and the world would, once again, be a place of promise. Something he had never imagined possible.

In this world, however, Lucy Forrester belonged to another man.

He'd ridden out into the desert, certain that it was Noor's memory he was running from. But alone, with only the stars for company, he'd discovered that it was Lucy who filled his thoughts.

No matter how hard he'd ridden, she had been at his back and he'd found no peace in sleep, but woke from disturbed dreams, his body hard, throbbing with raw desire, completely focused on a living, breathing woman for the first time since his world had fallen apart.

He'd come back determined to do what he should have done from the first—to move her to his mother's house or maybe ask Jamilla to take care of her until Zahir could organise her departure.

But he'd brought her here to appease some deep-seated need of his own. To help her and, in doing so, assuage his own desperate yearning for atonement.

How could he send her away now, because her presence disturbed his peace of mind? His mind deserved no peace…

'I'm sure Zahir is doing everything required,' he said. Although he was sure of nothing of the sort. He had not spoken to Zahir since he'd left for Rumaillah.

'If you could pass me my crutches?' Lucy prompted, sitting up, trying hard not to wince as her foot dragged on her ankle. 'Your lily pool is a joy to look at, but the mud is something else. I really need to go and wash it off.'

'Your sandals are ruined. I will fetch the wheelchair.'

'Okay, I'll reach them myself,' she said, pushing her good foot into a wet and muddy sandal and lifting herself using the arm of the sofa, swaying unsteadily as she kept one foot clear of the ground.

He reached out to steady her. Then, with his arm around her waist, he looked down at her and said, 'I should not have kissed you.'

'No,' she agreed, but her voice, as she continued, did not match her apparent carelessness. 'But then I really shouldn't have kissed you back. Why don't we forget it ever happened?'

As she turned to move away from the support of his arm, Han tried to imagine a world in which he could forget a kiss which, for one perfect moment, like the garden itself, had seemed to promise heaven on earth.

Lucy might, in law, belong to someone else, but she had kissed him as if he were the man she had been waiting for all her life and, in doing so, had delivered him from the past.

This was her place, her citadel, and he made a silent vow to himself that if Steve Mason had plans to reclaim his wife, he would have to wait on her convenience, her pleasure, make reparation for all the harm he'd done her, get on his knees and grovel for forgiveness before he would be allowed to cross the threshold. And then only to offer her the freedom to choose whether she left with him or stayed here, where she belonged.

Lucy had to force herself to move away from Han, from the support of his arm, even though all she wanted to do was lean against him, feel his arm at her back as she faced the future, but as she tried to ease clear, he tightened his grip.

'Han—'

Her voice rose in a cry of alarm as he bent and caught her behind the knees, lifting her into his arms and, dropping her crutches, she made a wild grab for his shoulders.

'I will do my best to forget that I kissed you, Lucy Forrester,' he said. 'That you kissed me.'

She was clutching at the cloth of his robe, bunching it beneath her hands, struggling for breath.

'Good,' she managed. 'Now, if you'll just put me down—'

'But as you told me so forcefully just a few days ago, memories become a part of us, make us what we are. Good and bad, we have to live with them.' He looked down at her, she thought, as if he was seeing her for the first time. 'We have to *live*.'

'I said that?' He did not reply. 'I said that,' she confirmed.

'Did you mean it?'

'Of course I meant it.' As if to demonstrate her sincerity, she stopped fighting the longing to let her arms wind themselves around his neck and let them have their way. 'I didn't think you were listening.'

'I did my best not to hear you,' he said, setting off with her, carrying her towards the pavilion. 'I rode like the wind, but your words kept pace with me. I tried to lose them, but there was nowhere to hide. Your words, your face when you want to be angry but you can't stop yourself from smiling, the scent of your skin as I washed you in the hospital—'

'Antiseptic,' she said, reliving a memory of her own. His irritation, his gentleness, his care…

'Antiseptic,' he agreed. 'Petrol fumes. Dust. The shampoo you'd used to wash your hair. Something else. Not scent…'

'Soap,' she said. 'I have this thing about really good soap. Gran used carbolic and it stung my face. I could never get away from the smell of it.' Even now, just to think of it brought back the smell, the roughness of the washcloth, and she buried her face in his shoulder. 'The first time I earned some money of my own, babysitting for a neighbour, I used it to buy good soap.'

'Your grandmother was harsh.'

'She did what she thought was right. She thought she'd failed with her daughter, wanted to save me from following in her footsteps. From the temptations of the flesh. The fact that I wanted expensive soap only proved to her how weak I was, strengthened her determination.'

He stopped. 'What did she do?'

'Nothing terrible. She just made me put it in a bowl of water, watch until it had completely dissolved and there was nothing left.'

'And yet you stayed, took care of her for all those years.'

'My teachers thought I was a fool. They wanted me to put her in a home, take my place at university. But she didn't do that to me, Han, even though it must have been hard for her to be left all on her own to bring up a baby. How could I leave when she needed me?'

'When you love someone you let them go, even when you need them more than life itself.'

That sounded, she thought, as if he was finally coming to terms with his loss. But despite the warmth of his body, of his arms, she shivered a little as he carried her out of the sunlight and into the blue shade of the arched walk.

Han picked up the phone, hit the fast dial for Zahir's cellphone. He should have returned days ago. He'd expected messages to be waiting for him. But there had been nothing.

The voice mail prompt cut in, asking him to leave a message. On the point of leaving one that was brief and to the point, he found himself distracted by the sight of a kitten scampering past the French window.

There were feral cats that lived wild around the stables, feeding off mice, but this was a pretty pedigree kitten, cream with a smudge on its nose and ears that would darken to chocolate and, if memory served him right, it would have blue eyes.

Abandoning the telephone, he followed the creature—creatures, there were two of them, he discovered—along the balcony, scooping up the pair of them in one hand before they could enter Lucy's sitting room.

She was lying back, her feet up, headphones

in place, oblivious to everything but the Arabic lessons she was repeating. He stood there, listening for a while, enjoying the sound of her cool English voice grappling with the unfamiliar sounds.

There was nothing half-hearted about her efforts. She was trying really hard and was clearly well along with her lessons. Determined, it seemed, to play a full part in the business she apparently half-owned.

He set one of the kittens down on the floor and watched as it ran to her, using its tiny claws to pull itself up on to her lap. She paused the CD player and, even though he couldn't see her face, he knew that she was smiling as she said, 'Hello, sweetie, where's your brother?' She turned to look for the kitten and saw Hanif.

She pulled off the headphones and said, 'Ah.'

The second kitten was wriggling desperately and he set it free to join its brother.

'I was going to tell you about the kittens.'

He didn't care about the kittens, but he envied them their freedom to rub against her, to demand her attention.

'Where did they come from?'

'Your sister. She phoned me and I asked if she could send some things to amuse Ameerah.'

'Did they?'

'Amuse her?' Her smile was rueful. 'For about five minutes. Then they wanted to sleep and when she wouldn't let them they scratched her.'

'Predictable, I would have thought. What else did she send?'

'A tricycle. Books. Games. Puzzles.'

'You seem to have kept yourself busy.' Then, because he knew his sister and because he had come to know Lucy too, he said, 'What else?'

'What makes you think there's something else?'

'Because, Lucy Forrester, your face gives away your every thought.'

'No…'

'It is true. You look at me and I know what you are thinking.' Even when her face was still, all expression blanked out, her eyes spoke volumes for those with the heart to read them. He should not be telling her that, but he could not help himself. He wanted her to know. To understand. 'Today,' he said, 'even when you were in pain, your only thought was for Ameerah. In your heart you were begging me to hold her close.'

She swallowed, gave a little shake of her head as if she found it disturbing to be so open to him, said, 'It was your own heart you were listening to, Han.' She quickly changed the subject. 'A Shetland pony arrived in a horsebox this morning, along with all the tack, riding clothes and a hard hat.' When he didn't say anything, she said, 'I'm sorry.'

'Don't be. You could have had no idea what forces you were unleashing.' Then, 'So, tell me, why is Ameerah chasing dragonflies instead of trotting around the garden on this fat little pony, giving Fathia palpitations and keeping a groom from his work?'

'I told Ameerah that the pony was tired from his journey.' Then, 'As you know, the Shetland Islands are a very, very long way from here.'

'And here I was thinking that Milly had off-loaded one of the ponies her own children had grown out of.'

'She might have done that,' Lucy said. 'I wasn't prepared to take the risk.'

He laughed. Laughed out loud. The sound was

rich and full and warmed Lucy's heart in a rush of joy. She had made him laugh and it was the most precious sound.

Then he reached for her hand and said, 'Don't go, Lucy.'

CHAPTER NINE

'DON'T go, Lucy. Stay here.'

Han was on his knees beside her, clasping her hands, and she could have no doubt what he was asking. He was offering her the citadel and she yearned to say yes, to take it, take him and all that he was offering.

When he'd kissed her, her response had been instinctive, without thought, without consideration of right or wrong, of what would follow. In his arms there had been no need to think.

Even the touch of his hands as they held hers was enough to drive all rational thought from her mind, tempt her in ways she could never have begun to imagine.

But she must think.

Not just for her own sake, but for his.

She had already made one terrible mistake, reaching back for the life she should have had when she was eighteen, desperately grabbing at a schoolgirl fantasy when she was a grown woman who should have long ago learned that life was not a fairy tale. But she'd learned nothing. She'd had no life. No chance to measure herself, make judgements, make mistakes, grow up.

How could she know whether this was real or just another fantasy, another crutch, so that she wouldn't have to face the reality of the life she'd been handed on the day her mother had abandoned her?

And maybe that was all she was for Hanif too. A crutch. Forced into such heightened intimacy, it was not surprising that he'd found himself responding to needs that he'd denied since Noor's death.

They'd both been living half lives for so long that they couldn't begin to know if what they felt was true emotion or simply the tingling of pins and needles as the blood began to flow back into unused muscles.

The heart, after all, was nothing more than a muscle. Wasn't it?

Unable to look at him, knowing that to look

up into his face was to signal surrender, she stared at their hands, linked together. His so strong, so beautiful. The hands of a horseman, a poet, a prince. Hers were the practical hands of a woman who had spent her life doing the kind of chores for which nails had to be kept short, that no amount of hand cream could ever keep soft.

Maybe Han had been right when he'd suggested she'd kept her hair long for herself. The one symbol of her femininity that no one could take from her.

He seemed to understand her instinctively, to know her every thought. Was that love?

Unable to help herself, she looked up, meeting eyes that seemed to assure her that it was. Found herself floundering, falling into their depths.

The kittens saved her, their needle-like claws jabbing her back to reality as they kneaded themselves a comfortable bed on her stomach.

'Ouch! Stop that!' she said, flustered, hot, confused.

Han, with his ability to read her thoughts, plainly understood that she had seized this excuse to avoid answering him.

Before she could say another word, he raised her hands to his lips, stepped back, bowed—not with the barest inclination of his head this time, but with his shoulders, his body, his hand to his heart—then, without uttering another word, he was gone.

She was right. Despite everything, Han thought—she was tied to another man and until she was free she could not pledge herself to him.

He might regret that, but he must honour her for doing what was right. Maybe it was time he did that too. Found Lucy's husband.

He called Zahir again and this time responded to the voice mail prompt. 'Find Mason. Bring him to me.'

Then, because he could not stay in the pavilion, because he did not want to go to the lodge, because he was restless and needed some distraction for a burning need that was in danger of consuming him, he went to the stables to see for himself what horror his sister had visited upon him.

And that was a mistake too.

Ameerah was there, grooming the already glossy

little pony under the eye of one of the grooms. With a silent gesture he sent the man away, took his place. She was so engrossed, chatting away happily to the pony as she brushed his thick cream mane, that she did not know he was there.

She was so like her mother that it hurt to look at her. Her gestures, the way she held her head to one side, the way her hair grew in soft curls.

She moved to the pony's forelock but, unable to reach, she turned to the groom for help. Froze as she saw him.

He could not speak, did not know what to say, but the pony snorted, nudged her in the back, and as she stumbled forward he caught her, picked her up. Knelt with her so that she was at the right height to finish grooming him.

'Tomorrow,' he said, before he set her down so that she could run to find Fathia, 'tomorrow I will teach you to ride.'

'Lucy! Lucy!'

It was early, the sun had barely risen above the mountains, but she was dressed as plainly as possible in a linen skirt that skimmed her ankles, a long-sleeved silk blouse.

Today she was leaving Rawdah al'-Arusah. It would, she thought, break her heart to leave, but it was impossible for her to stay.

After Han had left her she'd chosen to eat alone in her room shutting all the doors to keep out temptation. Closing herself away so he could not tempt her with a look that burned into her soul, or read her thoughts and know that she was lying when she said she wanted to leave.

Ameerah took no notice of closed doors. She burst in, a tiny dynamo in jodhpurs, ankle boots, a crisp white shirt and with her hair fastened up in a net under her velvet-covered hard hat.

'Come and watch me,' she begged, her eyes alight with happiness. 'I'm going to ride Moonlight!' The words came out in a jumble of Arabic and English but Lucy understood her perfectly. Then, as if sensing her hesitation, 'Pleeeease!'

How could she refuse? Besides, it was the one place she could guarantee not to meet Hanif. When she spoke to him she would have to be in total command of every one of her senses.

She followed Ameerah, moving swiftly now on her crutches. The extent of the stables should not have surprised her, but it did. There were boxes for dozens of horses around a paved yard as well as garaging for horseboxes and the powerful four-wheel drive vehicles required for desert travel.

'This way!'

Smiling, despite a sleepless night, a heavy heart, she allowed Ameerah to tug her in the direction of Moonlight's loose box. He was being saddled before being led out into the yard, a groom crouched low on his haunches so that he could tighten the girth.

Except that it wasn't a groom. As he straightened, towering over the tiny pony, she saw that it was Hanif and when he saw her he smiled.

'If I said that I can read your thoughts right now, Lucy Forrester, would you believe me?'

Shaking, weak with a confused mixture of feelings, she said, 'Believe me, at this moment even I do not know what I'm thinking.'

'Then I will tell you—'

'No!' The sting of tears that were both of joy and sadness cleared her mind as nothing else could have. 'I will not be responsible for any delay.' She tore herself away from the power of his gaze and turned to Ameerah. 'Your daughter will explode with excitement if she has to wait another moment.'

'She and I have that in common.'

Before she could respond, he turned to Ameerah, lifting his little girl into the saddle, adjusting the stirrups for her, showing her how to hold the reins. Then, because the attention span of a three-year-old was limited, he led her slowly around the yard so that everyone could see how wonderful she looked, before taking the pony for a walk down a shady path.

Lucy did not follow—this was a time for father and daughter. Turning to go, she found herself confronted by Fathia.

'You really are leaving today, Lucy?'

'I have to.'

'Hanif will miss you.'

'He has his daughter. In a few weeks he will rediscover his life.'

The woman took her hand and patted it, whether with sympathy or gratitude, she could not have said. 'Go to the summer house, Lucy. I will send him to you so that you can say goodbye.'

* * *

A light breeze was blowing across the pool, cooling the summer house. A servant brought coffee, freshly baked croissants, a bowl of fresh figs.

After a while Hanif joined her and she poured coffee for them both, handed a cup to him. He took it, capturing her fingers so that she could not let go.

'So, Lucy, you have decided to leave us?'

'Is that what you read in my thoughts?'

'Not just that.'

No. Caught off guard her thoughts must have blazed like a beacon. 'You no longer need me, Hanif.'

He smiled at that. 'You stayed for my sake?'

'I asked to leave days ago,' she reminded him. She'd spent a long and sleepless night thinking about what she would say to him. 'I have to go, Hanif.' She swallowed, forced herself to continue. 'But there are some things I have to ask you before I leave.'

He released her hand, put down the cup.

'Do not ask anything for this man you married—'

'No! Not for him.' He waited. 'Steve was living

with a woman in Rumaillah. Jenny Sanderson. She's the office manager of Bouheira Tours. She's expecting a baby very soon…'

Lucy struggled to continue, remembering that moment when she'd walked into the office, introduced herself, said, 'Hi, I'm Lucy Mason. I'm looking for my husband…'

She hadn't needed the 'couple' photographs pinned to the notice-board to warn her. The look on Jenny Sanderson's face had been enough to tell her whose baby she was carrying.

Han said something beneath his breath, but it was not anything she was meant to hear or understand and she didn't ask him to repeat it.

'How long ago did he marry you, Lucy? Weeks? How many months has this woman been carrying his child?'

'He must have been desperate for money, in real trouble, Hanif, but she and her baby have done nothing.'

He didn't leap to agree, but he let it go, said, 'What do you want me to do for her?'

'She may need support and I'm not sure that Steve can provide it. Maybe money to get home.

I don't know if the company is worth anything, or if the papers that give me a half share in it are valid, but if a buyer can be found I'd like to use that money to give her a fresh start.'

'Let me tell you something, Lucy. This woman, for whom you feel such empathy, is the person who denied you existed. If I had not been near, if you had run out of fuel so far from the track, you could have died.'

'What do you mean, far from the track?'

'You were headed to Mason's camp in the foothills of the mountains?'

'Well, yes…'

'You were miles off track, headed into empty wilderness. The satellite navigation system on the 4x4 was malfunctioning.'

He saw her take in what he'd told her, the colour leave her face. 'How do you know that?'

'Zahir has spent the last few days piecing together exactly what happened. He called me last night. Jenny Sanderson thought you were dead and to cover for this man she had someone drive out and collect the burnt out 4x4, take it away to be crushed.'

Lucy gripped the arm of the chair for a moment,

then forced herself to say, 'She was protecting her baby, Han. A woman will do anything…'

She stopped. The air was as fragile as glass. One word, the wrong word, could shatter it.

'You would forgive her anything?' Han said.

'Please, Han.'

Han had known from the moment he had stood up and seen her in the stable that she was ready to leave. She had convinced herself that it was the right thing to do. And seeing him with Ameerah had only made it easier for her.

If the pain of losing her was not enough to convince him that he loved her, the compassion she could show for another of Mason's victims left him in no doubt. He did not believe the woman deserved a second thought, but he could deny her nothing.

'Very well, Lucy. If you can forgive, then I must too. I'll see that she comes to no harm.' He regarded her for a moment. 'What about Mason?'

'What about him?'

'He is your husband. Having disposed of the pregnant girlfriend, is it your intention to return to him?'

The question had to be faced; he knew she

was the kind of woman who would always honour a promise, keep a vow.

'Is that what a good Ramal Hamrah girl would do?' she asked, surprising him.

'A good Ramal Hamrah girl would hunt him down and cut out his treacherous heart,' he assured her. 'But your marriage was not arranged, it was a love match. As you have just proved, a woman in love will forgive anything…'

'Hanif…'

She said his name and he saw a reflection of what she must see in his eyes.

'Lucy…'

If he did not look away, if he could hold her, like this, locked in his eyes, she could not leave him…

'Lucy…' The voice became more insistent and with a sigh she turned away from him to look at the man she'd married. The man who'd so cruelly cheated not only her but the woman who was carrying his child.

'Oh, my God, look at the state of you! Your face…'

Mason reached out as if to touch her and it was all Hanif could do to stop himself from slamming him back against the trunk of the nearest tree.

'My apologies, Excellency,' Zahir said quickly. 'I was told you were here. I assumed you were alone.'

Hanif rose to his feet, waving away his apology. 'I did not hear the helicopter.'

'There is a *shamal* blowing down the coast. We had to come by road.'

He nodded, turned to confront the man. 'You have something to say, Mason?'

'Your Highness,' he said, bowing, 'Thou who hast long life. I can do nothing but offer the humblest of thanks for rescuing Lucy. For taking care of her.'

His contempt for the man knew no bounds. Did he think to charm him with formal greetings, smooth words?

'Not to me. To your wife.'

Lucy stared, first at Hanif who had, before her eyes, it seemed, morphed from the gentlest of lovers into the most aloof of autocrats, then at Steve, blathering nonsense in an attempt to ingratiate himself with Hanif.

Embarrassed for him, she said, 'Save the apologies.' Then, as he opened his mouth to say something, no doubt some well rehearsed story that was meant to melt her heart, but she'd had enough of his lies, 'Just tell me why you did it.'

It was strange. Now she knew he was lying she could see what he was doing, recognised the exact moment when he realised that the truth would serve him better. The subtle rearrangement of his expression from humble penitent to frankness and honesty.

'You're right. You deserve an explanation.'

Lucy made no comment on what she deserved, simply waited for him to continue.

'I came to England to try and raise some finance for the business. I needed capital, but no one here would back me. My last hope was that my parents would raise a loan on their house. It's a brilliant business, Luce—'

'Lucy,' she snapped, cringing at the familiarity of a diminutive that she'd once thought meant something. 'My name is Lucy.'

'Lucy,' he repeated.

She waved him on and Han found himself having to hide a smile. Not one of his sisters could have done it with more authority, more disdain, he thought.

'It's a brilliant business,' Mason repeated,

now less certain of himself. 'There are endless possibilities. The desert is the last great tourist destination…'

'But you are not a great credit risk, are you?' Zahir said, cutting him short. 'This isn't the first business you've tried. You take short cuts. You have no staying power.'

Mason looked for a moment as if he was going to protest, but finally he shook his head.

'No. Even my parents turned me down. I was going into town to book my flight back when I saw the For Sale sign up outside your house, Lucy. My mother had mentioned that your gran had died and I realised that she must have left you the house.'

'I was surprised you remembered me. School was a long time ago.'

'Oh, please. All those brains. All that hair. It was a matter of considerable debate whether, if you cut your hair, you'd lose the power of thought. The way that Samson lost his strength.'

'And no one thought to corner me somewhere, cut it off, to find out?'

He looked embarrassed. Probably a first, Han thought.

'You had something about you, even then, Lucy. We were all a bit in awe, to be honest.'

Han saw her eyes, felt the loneliness of the girl she'd been, saw her rally as she realised that this was no more than a ploy to gain her sympathy.

'Not that much in awe, obviously,' she said. 'You let me keep my hair, but my money was something else.'

'I always meant to pay you back. You have to believe that. I thought I'd be able to pay off the cards, or at least some of them, before you ever knew.'

'And the bank loan?' Han interjected, growing impatient. 'When were you going to repay that?'

'I intended to pay off the first instalment. Once I'd done that I was going to explain everything,' he said, turning to Lucy with all the natural confidence of a man who believed all he had to do was smile. That something would always turn up to save him. 'Cash flow is the killer.'

'Not quite as deadly as a malfunctioning satellite navigation system in the desert,' Zahir suggested.

'Look, Jenny didn't know Lucy had taken the 4x4. She'd left it for the garage to pick up. It was only when you called that she realised what had happened. She called me in the most terrible state. She thought Lucy was dead.'

'So you told her to collect the burned out vehicle, have it crushed and no one would ever be able to prove anything.'

He drew a breath. 'No. I organised that. I panicked…'

'She told Zahir that she had done it.'

'She was protecting me.'

'More fool her,' he said.

Lucy caught his eye. *A woman will do anything…*

'I did give you half the company, Lucy, and there are bookings. Zahir will tell you. He's seen the books. Seen everything. I was desperate for capital. I needed more equipment, better transport, a decent website. Time. Give me a chance and I will repay you every penny and more.'

'It is true, Excellency. The money he took has certainly been ploughed into the business and there appears to be no shortage of people who want what Bouheira Tours is offering.'

Han could almost feel Zahir's excitement, enthusiasm.

'Han?' Lucy prompted.

He had thought it a blessing, a treasure, to be able to read Lucy's thoughts, but now he saw all too clearly what she wanted. Mercy.

He didn't want to breathe the same air as this man and yet he appeared to expect to be treated as a businessman rather than the criminal he undoubtedly was.

'You plead for him? When he has betrayed you in every way a man can betray a woman?'

'I'm not pleading for him.' She reached out, didn't quite touch his hand. 'I ask your mercy for the girl who loves him, her unborn baby.'

'You ask me to allow this man to remain in Ramal Hamrah? Polluting my country with his presence?'

'If he is ever to repay me, the company has to be made to pay.'

'Pay? You believe he will repay you?'

'If I have to stand over him with a whip.'

'You will stay? Work with him?'

Live with him?

Never, while he had breath in his body and, recalling her compassion for a wife who had to share her husband, he used it shamelessly.

'You are prepared to share him?' he demanded. 'Play the role of the second wife? Counting the baubles. Keeping watch to make sure he does not visit his girlfriend more often than he visits you.'

He turned away before he saw her answer in her eyes.

Why wouldn't she? Hadn't Lucy told him, over and over, that a woman would do anything, not just for her child, but for the man she loved? He recognised that he was being given a second chance to prove that he could do as much for a woman who had given him back the capacity not just to love, but to live, no matter how much it cost him.

'Actually…'

They all turned to Mason.

'The thing is that Jenny…' All the colour had leached from his skin, leaving him looking yellow rather than fit and tanned and his voice was less than steady. 'I'm sorry, Lucy, but she's not my girlfriend, she's my wife.' He looked terrible, but even so he seemed to be standing a little taller, looking more of a man. 'The thing is I love her. I'd do anything for her.' Shrugged. 'Have done just about anything…'

Lucy's face was expressionless and, for the first time since their eyes had met in the split second before she'd passed out on him, Han didn't have the slightest idea what she was thinking.

No one prompted Mason, demanded answers. They all simply waited.

'The emergency that called me back here straight after the wedding ceremony was a fake, Lucy. All that flap about getting a seat on a plane was just so much window-dressing. I already had my flight booked.'

'Am I supposed to thank you for that?'

'No. It wasn't that you aren't lovely, Lucy. Any man would be proud…'

'But you loved Jenny too much to be unfaithful to her?'

He nodded. 'I sort of surprised myself. I guess I must have some standards—'

'Standards?' Han demanded, quite certain that this was nothing more than a ploy for sympathy. 'Isn't bigamy a criminal offence?'

'Not one that gets taken very seriously these days. The worst I'm likely to get is a caution.'

'You checked it out, did you? I think you might be just a little optimistic; I've no idea what we do with bigamists in Ramal Hamrah, but we do take fraud very seriously.'

'He has a wife, Han, and a baby on the way. I'd already talked to a lawyer about a divorce, but now I can get an annulment. That's all I want.' Lucy's voice was trembling a little, as if she'd been under a tremendous strain and suddenly it was over.

'Divorce?'

She gave an awkward little shrug. 'I'm sorry, Han, you're going to have a heck of a telephone bill and it appears that I haven't, after all, got a husband for you to send it to.'

Her words, her face were solemn enough, but her eyes... Her lovely silver eyes were smiling.

'If you say one word about paying for it yourself,' he warned, 'I shall have to insist that you marry me.'

He'd thought he'd been losing his mind, but even when he'd thought her married he'd seen the innocence shining from her. He hadn't needed Mason to tell him that he had not touched this wife, had not stolen from her the one thing that he could never return.

It occurred to him that everyone was staring at him and he turned to Zahir.

'Miss Forrester wishes to sell her half of
Bouheira Tours, Zahir. As a graduate of Harvard
Business School and a keen advocate of our bur-
geoning tourist industry, it seems to me that you
might be interested in investing in such a
venture.'

'I would be delighted to have such a partner,'
Mason began.

'I'm sure you would,' Han said, cutting him
short. 'However, the State of Ramal Hamrah does
not allow felons to profit from their crimes. Your
assets will be confiscated and sold to repay your
creditors, of whom, I'm sure, there are many.'

'You're going to deport me?'

He looked, Han thought, almost indignant.

'Deport you? On the contrary. We will deport
your wife. Pregnant or not, she was a party to
your crime. A willing accomplice—'

'Han! You promised!'

'—but you, Mason, will remain in Ramal
Hamrah until our courts decide what to do with
you.'

'Han, please!'

'Do not plead for him, Lucy. This man stole
your money, very nearly stole your life. He's full

of remorse now, but if I let him walk away, how long do you think it will be before he's cruelly abusing the trust of some other vulnerable woman, stealing her money and destroying her life in the process, now that he knows how easy it is? How reluctant she would be to press charges. Are you prepared to take the responsibility for that?'

Her eyes blazed at him. 'You promised me that you would take care of Jenny Sanderson.'

'I will. She'll be repatriated at my expense, which is rather more than she was prepared to do for you.' She turned away, furious with him. Or more probably furious with herself. The fact that she somehow felt guilty for their crimes was one of the nastiest things about this. 'Zahir, after you've delivered Mr Mason to the relevant authorities, I suggest you take immediate control of Bouheira Tours. We can't have our tourists left stranded.'

'Excellency...' The boy seemed unable to speak. Totally overcome. 'His Highness the Emir, your father...'

'I will be returning to Rumaillah, Zahir. Your duty here is done.'

CHAPTER TEN

Lucy stared out of the window at an aircraft taxiing towards the terminal building. Anywhere but at Han.

She'd stayed with Milly while her papers had been organised, been introduced to Hanif's mother, his grandmother, and received with the utmost courtesy.

Did they have any idea of the trouble she'd been in? How much Hanif had done for her? She couldn't ask him. She hadn't seen him since she'd been left in Milly's care. According to his sister, he was spending all his time with his father.

'They're discussing Han's future,' she said.

'Future?' It was none of her business, she knew, but she couldn't stop herself.

'He's resuming his diplomatic career, going to the UN as a special envoy to the commission on world poverty.'

'The UN?' New York? That was so far away…
'And Ameerah?' she managed.

Milly smiled. 'He's taking her with him.'

Relief swept through her. It would have been so easy for him to leave her behind. 'She must be so happy.'

'Yes.' Milly's smile faded. 'Noor was brought up in an old-fashioned household where girls were not valued. She didn't understand that our father, our brothers…' She shook her head. 'Every time that Hanif looked at Ameerah he remembered that Noor had lied to him, that she couldn't bring herself to totally trust him. We are all so grateful for what you've done, Lucy.'

'It was nothing. He saved my life.'

Milly reached out, took her hand, squeezed it.

'I think the honours are about even.' She turned at the sound of footsteps crossing the hall, 'It's time to go. Have you got everything?'

'Yes…' And without warning she found herself looking at Hanif for the first time since they'd parted in anger. 'I'm just leaving,' she said stupidly.

'I know. Ameerah and I have come to take you to the airport.'

'Oh.'

Of course. How foolish to think that he had come to ask her to stay. He was leaving too. Reclaiming his life, as she must reclaim hers.

The little girl grabbed her attention in the car, chatting all the way to the airport, telling her about going to New York.

It was only after they had been ushered through to the luxury of a private lounge, when Ameerah had been distracted by the planes, that they had a chance to speak.

'You are still angry with me, Lucy?'

'Angry?'

'You believe I treated Mason harshly?' She gave an awkward little shrug. 'He has to learn that his actions have consequences, Lucy.'

'Then maybe I should be in prison too.' She turned and regarded him levelly. 'I wanted the fantasy. To be the kind of girl that a boy like Steve Mason would notice. If I hadn't been so needy, so pathetic, he wouldn't have been able to fool me. He wouldn't be in jail.'

'You are not needy, Lucy. No one has a more giving or warmer nature than you.' He took her hands. 'Too good for the world, maybe. I do not think I should let you go back to the world. I should keep you in my garden with the other flowers, where you will be safe.'

She shook her head, tried to pull away, but he would not let her go.

Han wanted to hold her, keep her safe, offer her all the fantasies she'd ever dreamed of. But she had taught him that when you loved someone, you had to let them fly. Take the risk that they might not ever return.

'I'm not a flower,' she said.

'Are you sure? You have all the attributes of the rose, including the thorns.'

'What will happen to that poor woman and her baby?'

'Jenny Sanderson? Why do you care more about her than yourself?' he demanded. He did not want to talk about them, or the past. He wanted to talk about the future.

'It could have been me,' she said desperately, wanting him to understand. 'I feel responsible.'

'No, Lucy. They are responsible for what they did. They must face the consequences of their actions, as we all must.'

'You once said that you could refuse me nothing.'

And, God help him, he had meant it.

'Not this. On this I am adamant.' Then, because he could not help himself. 'Do you have to go?'

'I have to sell the house, Han. Settle my debts. Find a life that's my own. Not a prison, not some fantasy, but something real.'

This is real, he wanted to say. What I feel, what I know you feel…

She lifted her head a little. 'I'm going to try and get a university place as a mature student.'

'You want to take your degree in French literature?'

'No, I'm not that girl any more. I've been thinking about what I'll do…'

She seemed about to say something, but changed her mind about sharing it with him. He didn't press her, but said, 'What about your mother? Will you look for her?'

She nodded, apparently unable to speak.

'If there is anything I can do to help, Lucy…' Before he could say what was in his heart, a steward arrived to inform them that Lucy's flight was boarding.

'One moment.'

But Lucy had already detached herself, was on her feet, burying her face in Ameerah's hair. 'Goodbye, my darling. Have a lovely life.'

Then, having composed herself, she turned to him.

'Thank you, Han.' She offered him her hand. 'For my life. For everything. I will never forget you.'

He recognised the gesture for what it was. It was how the British said goodbye. Not just goodbye for now, but good-bye for ever.

He ignored it, taking not one, but both of her hands, holding them against his chest, willing her to understand that while he'd learned the lesson about letting go, for him this was not goodbye, only a necessary pause while they put what had happened into the perspective of their everyday lives. Time for him to rebuild his life, for her to reach out for the life she'd never had.

There were a thousand things he wanted to say to her, but he recognised that she wasn't ready to trust herself with the kind of decisions, commitments, such declarations would demand. Instead he kissed both of her cheeks before raising her hands to his lips.

'*Ma'as salamah,* Lucy. Go, in the safety of Allah.'

'*Ma'as salamah,* Han…'

Lucy wanted to say more. To let him see that she understood that this was an end. That they came from different worlds and that whatever he'd said, done, she understood that once he had returned to his real life she would become nothing more than a memory. A sweet memory, she hoped, a memory to raise a smile long after he'd forgotten what she looked like, struggled to remember her name.

But her throat was constricted and the words wouldn't come. It didn't matter. A week, a month, from now and he would discover it for himself.

All she could do was grab her crutches and follow the steward assigned to take her to her seat, but as she reached the door Ameerah raced after her to give her a last hug, clutching at her legs, holding her there.

Han said something to the child and she let go, ran back to him, lifted her arms. There was no hesitation now as he bent, picked her up. No un-certainty as Ameerah wrapped her arms about his neck and buried her head in his shoulder.

She had done that.

If she did nothing else in her life, Lucy would always cherish the thought that she had once managed to unite a little girl with her father.

Their eyes met one last time over Ameerah's head. His lips moved but a tannoy announcement drowned out his words. It didn't matter, there was nothing left to say, and with a brief nod she turned, boarded the truck that was waiting to carry her to the aircraft.

She'd had a lifetime of keeping her feelings hidden, kept tightly locked away. Her throat was tight, aching, she could barely speak to thank the steward after he'd carried her flight bag upstairs, installed her in the luxury of the royal suite on the upper deck of the Ramal Hamrah airliner.

It was the last word in luxury. It had armchairs, a fully functioning office with every communications device known to man, even a bedroom, should she choose to sleep.

But it was the book waiting by her seat that really undid her.

Han's own volume of the poems of Hafiz, inscribed on the flyleaf—'So that you will not forget'. He had signed it, not in English, but in looping Arabic script.

Any girl would cry.

As Han watched the airliner lift off from the runway, he felt for one desperate moment as if he was losing his heart for the second time.

'Where has Lucy gone, Daddy?'

He looked down at the child in his arms.

No.

It wasn't like that. A heart that was fully functioning, beating soundly, had an infinite capacity to expand, to fill many places, many time zones.

It might be lifting at that moment with Lucy, being torn from him as the plane lifted her six miles above the earth, but it was here too, on the ground with his daughter.

It resided, he realised in a sudden flash of insight, with everyone one had ever loved.

In the past with those who had gone to paradise. In the present with family, friends, all those who cared for you, who you cared for in return. With all the possibilities of the future.

Lucy, whose boundless love had been constrained and cramped in a joyless life, had nevertheless endless compassion for a woman who had not loved her as she deserved. Empathy for two people who would have stolen her life if she had not had the courage to come and take it back.

She'd had love to spare for a small mother-less child and even a little left over for a lonely, half-dead man.

Now she was going to find the mother who'd abandoned her and he had no doubt that she would find it in her heart to forgive her, love her too if she had the courage to cherish the gift of a daughter.

'Where has she *gone,* Daddy?' Ameerah per-sisted.

'She's gone to a place called England. It's very green. Very beautiful.'

'Why has she gone there?'

'She has some things she has to do.' As he did. A life to resurrect, a family to spend time with, a country that needed him. He owed his father three years of duty. He'd asked only for three months.

'Will she come and see us soon?'

'*In sha'Allah,* my sweet.' If God wills.

Life, Lucy quickly discovered, was not as diffi-cult as she'd imagined.

For the best part of twenty-eight years she'd clung to a small core of resistance, keeping a part of herself inviolate from the buffeting of a life that hadn't handed her any easy options. At school she'd learned to keep her head down, avoid trouble and reach the goals she'd set herself. Since then, she'd had ten years of dealing with Social Services, the medical profession, her increasingly frail grandmother.

Steve had caught her at the one moment when she'd had her guard down; when she'd stopped fighting; when it had seemed that, finally, it was to be her turn and he'd taken pitiless advantage of her at a vulnerable moment. Han had been right; once he'd realised just how easy it was he'd do it again in a heartbeat.

She wished she could tell him.

Explain that once she was back in England and faced with sorting out the mess, confronting the true horror of what Steve had done, she'd understood why he'd acted the way he had.

As for Jenny Sanderson, Zahir had forwarded a letter from her, telling her how sorry she was for what she'd done. That she felt as if she'd been woken up from some drugged dream in which she'd been sleepwalking into danger. How grateful she was to be back home with parents who loved her, were eagerly looking forward to the arrival of a grandchild. The chance to make a fresh start.

It was a fresh start all round, it seemed. Having put the house back on the market, she'd wasted no time in taking herself to an employment agency to see what kind of job she might get. A bit of an eye-opener, that one.

'What qualifications do you have, Lucy?'

'None. I'm not expecting anything more than the basic wage,' she admitted. 'I've no experience, you see. I've never had anything but holiday jobs. I've been caring for my grandmother for the last ten years…'

Even as she said the words she realised that she was simply repeating what Steve had told her, using her insecurities to bind her to him.

'Scrub that. I've got twelve O levels, four A levels, I've spent the last ten years running a house on a pittance and dealing with Social Services in all its forms. I speak passable

French, can get by in Italian and I'm learning Arabic. Oh, and I can drive.'

'French?' The woman smiled. 'How are your computer skills?'

Computer skills... Her confidence ebbed. 'I haven't used a computer since I was at school.'

'Don't worry, we'll give you a crash course on the latest software this afternoon. That's if you're free to start a temp job tomorrow?' She smiled. 'At considerably more than the basic rate.'

After a couple of days, when she discovered that common sense and the ability to knuckle down and get the work done were just as valuable as her ability to answer the telephone confidently in French—and not panic when the caller replied in the same language—made her a very valuable commodity indeed. The only thing that she lacked was someone to tell.

There was, she discovered, a great big Han-shaped void at the centre of her life. Just how big a hole that was she'd only discovered when she got home from work one day and turned on the little television set she'd bought herself, to catch the end of the evening news.

She'd switched on in the middle of a report from the UN on international aid and, without warning, she was looking at the impressive figure of Sheikh Hanif al-Khatib as he addressed the Assembly. He looked, she thought, like a man who had the world by the throat. Strong. Passionate. Alive in every sense of the word.

Alive and so far away.

She'd pressed her hand against the screen, faint with longing to be near him. In the same room as him. In the same country...

She relived every moment of the time they'd spent together, her anger, that last moment when his words had been drowned out by the speaker system. And suddenly she knew what he'd said. *'Call me...'*

And say what? *I miss you. I love you...*

Or was that simply *I need you?*

Was she still looking for a prop?

She did miss him, she did love him, but she had to prove to them both that the only person she *needed* was herself.

She applied for a place at the School of

Oriental and African Studies in London. The temporary job at the international finance company had become permanent but she had bigger ambitions. With her languages and a degree in Arabic Cultural Studies she could aspire to a post at the Foreign Office, join the Diplomatic Service. Get a job at the United Nations…

That would be a Life.

Then, to stop herself thinking about Han, she turned to the one thing she'd been putting off and searched out the name of the agency where she could register to find her mother.

'I'll take the details, Lucy,' the counsellor told her. 'But I don't hold out much hope that we can help. You weren't adopted so there won't be any records.'

'No. I understand.' And she understood the unspoken subtext—that if her mother had wanted to find her, all she had to do was go back to where she'd left her.

'Maybe you could try an Internet search? There is a website where families can get in touch. It's basically for genealogy, but it would be a start and if that doesn't come up with anything, well, you could just type her name into a search engine and see what you come up with.'

She did both. The Internet came back with 654,000 hits for Elizabeth Forrester.

After a quick look at some of them, she realised that she'd got every Elizabeth and every Forrester in the entire world. And that the Elizabeths were not necessarily connected to the Forresters.

She refined her search details and tried again. And again. When she'd reduced the number of hits to three, she sent each of them the same email.

Are you Elizabeth Forrester, the daughter of Jessica Forrester, who once lived in Maybridge? Lucy.

She didn't give a street address. Her mother would know it. A fake would not.

Her job, the discovery that she had skills people were willing to pay for, that she could make friends—Deena, the Jordanian student she'd found through the university who was teaching her Arabic script, people she worked with—was giving her confidence.

Life was teaching her caution.

Parties, concerts, diplomatic functions... Han stripped off and stood beneath the shower to wash away the latest round of polite and meaningless conversation.

Three months...

After yet another reception fending off the attentions of women who hoped to bag themselves a sheikh to add to the notches on their bedposts, of forcing himself to be polite to the front men of dictators who let their people starve while they lined their pockets at the expense of the poor, a day without Lucy was beginning to feel like a lifetime.

If she had been with him to share the horrors, make him laugh at the foolishness of it all, make it all go away with the sweetness of her mouth, the tenderness of her touch...

He wrapped a towel around his waist, crossed the bedroom to the telephone, picked up the receiver, wanting more than anything in the world to hear her voice.

He held it for a moment, then quietly replaced

it. He had told her to call him. When she was ready, when nothing else was possible, he had to believe she would, trust her to do that.

Lucy heard from her solicitor that her marriage had been officially annulled. Was as if it had never happened. Which, in every way that counted, it never had.

To celebrate she took her nails, growing strongly now, to have them manicured in a new nail bar in town and after that, she paid a long delayed visit to the hairdresser.

'How much do you want me to take off?' the girl asked.

Lucy thought about it. Thought about all the times she'd dreamed of this moment, then, realising that she had nothing to prove, no one to please but herself, said, 'Just as much as it takes to straighten up the ends, please.'

The family genealogy Internet site, on which she'd carefully entered her limited family tree, had not produced any results. She'd two negative replies to her emails, both of them wishing her luck with her search, which left just one Elizabeth Forrester to answer. Was it her mother? Was she some respectable woman who had wiped out the past and was even now living in fear and trembling that her daughter was about to turn up and destroy her neatly ordered life?

She wrote again.

If you are Elizabeth Forrester, formerly of Maybridge, if you are my mother, all I want is…

She stopped. She didn't know what she wanted. Everything. Nothing. To hear her voice. Look her in the eyes and see… What?

She deleted the message.

A month passed and still there was no answer from Elizabeth Forrester number three.

Suppose her email had not arrived? Was it still buzzing around somewhere in cyberspace? It had happened at work only the other day and a deal had nearly fallen through…

She wrote again.

I am looking for my mother, Elizabeth
Forrester, daughter of Jessica Forrester of
Maybridge. Please, if it's not you, will you
let me know so that I can cross you off my
list? Lucy Forrester.

She hit 'send', then stared at the screen as if
expecting a reply to drop into her mailbox.

'A watched computer never delivers mail,'
Deena told her. 'Come on, let's go to the super-
market, I'll make you some *khoushaf.*'

The distraction worked until Lucy saw the
fresh figs on display, cold, hard, a world away
from the soft, sweet fruit she'd shared with Han.
She told an unconvinced Deena that she had a
headache, went home and took out the kaftans
Han had bought for her, rubbing the silk against
her cheek, imagining some faint lingering scent
of roses, remembering Ameerah's face as she'd
paraded herself in the *shalwar kameez.*

Picked up the poetry book he'd given her and
held it against her heart, wondering what he'd be
doing at that moment in New York.

Was he at some diplomatic cocktail party surrounded by countless women, all of them cleverer than her, prettier, dressed in the kind of clothes that a man like Han would expect a woman worth his attention to wear?

Then she realised that she was still doing it. Despite her good job, the place she'd won at SOAS, the friends she'd made, she hadn't moved on where it mattered. In her head she knew that she was a strong, bright woman who deserved everything that life had to offer, but in her heart she still believed that because her mother hadn't wanted her, she wasn't worth anything.

The next day she placed advertisements in the personal columns of all the national newspapers, appealing for information. Contacted the local radio station and used their 'find a friend' request programme. She was even interviewed by the local newspaper.

She hated every minute of it. It was like exposing herself in public. Walking naked down the street in slow motion.

And it was all for nothing. Worse than nothing. The only responses she had were from desperate women looking for their own children, desperate children looking for their mothers, all of them wanting to share their own stories.

At least she'd finally managed to sell the house, get that burden off her back, clear her debts.

She moved into a flat share with one of her colleagues from work, learned how to head off the invitations to drinks, dinner, the movies from the men she met. Not because they weren't decent men, not because she didn't trust her own judgement, but because they weren't Han.

Then one evening when she got home from work there was a woman standing on the pavement looking up at the first floor windows as if she'd knocked, had got no answer, but still hoped that there might be someone home.

'Can I help?' Lucy asked. 'Who are you looking for?' But even before the words were out of her mouth, she knew.

She'd seen photographs of her grandmother as a young woman. Had seen her own face in the mirror countless times. This woman was both of them, neither of them, unknown and yet recognised in ways that went to the deepest part of the soul.

Lucy just stood there, unable to move, to speak…

'I went to the house,' her mother said. 'The woman who lives there gave me the name of the estate agent who sold it to her. I thought they might know where you were. I was going to ask them to send on a letter.' She made a vague wordless gesture. 'One of the women there told me where to find you. She said you'd want her to…'

Someone else arrived, opened the door, held it for a moment and then, when neither of them moved, let it swing shut.

Still Lucy stood there.

'Maybe she was wrong. I'll understand if you don't want to see me, talk to me…' She turned, began to move, but Lucy reached out, laid her hand on her mother's arm, kept her from walking away, finally managed to say, 'No. Please. I've been looking for you.'

'Looking for me?'

Lucy saw hope in her mother's face and all the years fell away.

'For months. I used local radio, newspapers, the Internet…'

'I've been living abroad. New Zealand. My husband knew nothing about you until a few months ago when I had a bit of a scare. A lump in my breast.' She shook her head. 'No. It wasn't, but for a while I thought I might die and that I'd never have known you… I told Michael everything and he brought me home to confront my mother, to demand to know where she'd placed you so that I could begin to look for you.'

'Placed me?'

Her mother struggled to speak. 'She took you away from the hospital, told me you'd been given to a good God-fearing couple who couldn't have children, that they were going to adopt you, take you away, that I'd never see you again. That it was best.' Tears were pouring down her cheeks. 'Everyone said it was for the best.'

'But she didn't,' Lucy said. 'She raised me herself.'

'She kept you?' Her mother stifled a cry of anguish with her hand. It was a cry, Lucy realised with an overwhelming sense of her loss, that she'd been stifling all her life. 'I never went back. I walked out of the hospital and never went back. I never wanted to see or speak to her ever again. I couldn't forgive her. Bear to be in the same house, the same room...'

She put out a hand as if to touch Lucy, but couldn't quite bring herself to bridge the gap in case she was not real, only some figment of her imagination.

'If I'd come back, just once, I could have been with you. I could have borne anything to be with you...'

'Don't,' Lucy said, reaching out as her mother had. Not quite touching. 'Please, Mum...'

And then, somehow, without either of them knowing how it happened, they were in each other's arms, holding each other, weeping and laughing.

It was being with her mother, discovering that she had a wonderful stepfather, a sixteen-year-old half-sister, had been given the family she'd always longed for, that made her realise that finding a life was nowhere near as important as living the life you'd been handed. Being with the people you loved. That the risk of looking a fool was nowhere near as bad as being one and losing something unbelievably precious.

On a Monday afternoon, a month after she'd been reunited with her mother, she picked up her cellphone and called the United Nations building in New York, asked to speak to Sheikh Hanif al-Khatib.

She was put through to his office. His secretary was polite. 'Sheikh Hanif is not expected in the office today, Miss Forrester. Do you wish to leave a message?'

Having screwed herself up to make the call, disappointment flooded through her.

'Tell him I called, will you?'

Then, even before she'd hung up, she was summoned to the Chairman's office and, before she knew it, she was on a plane to Paris.

'Are you doing anything tonight, Lucy?' one of her colleagues asked as they went down in the lift.

'Forget it, Jamie. After that Paris trip, she's holding out for the boss.'

'I think she's got bigger ambitions than that,' someone else chipped in as the doors opened and they headed for the door.

'Bigger? What's bigger than that?'

'Royalty.'

Lucy, who had until that moment ignored the usual banter, turned and stared at the girl who'd spoken.

'What are you talking about?'

'I took a phone call for you from some bloke who said he was a sheikh. While you were away.'

Lucy felt her knees buckle. She'd come back from Paris hoping that Hanif would have called back. When she found out he hadn't...

'I didn't get any message. When did he ring?'

'Come on, it was a wind-up,' the girl said. Then, 'Tuesday, Wednesday. I left a note on your desk.'

'It wasn't there when I got back this morning.'

'Hey, don't fret,' Jamie said. 'I'm short a white stallion but I can whisk you away in a BMW coupé—'

'Black,' she said, cutting him short as she punched the lift button to call it back so that she could go and search for the message. 'The stallion has to be black.'

'Black. Right.' Then, 'Is that your way of telling me that there's no point in asking you out for a drink?'

'No point whatever,' she assured him, but none of the men were listening. They were all too busy crowding through the door to drool over the black Aston Martin parked in front of the entrance.

From her place by the lift Lucy saw the door open, the driver step out. He was dressed casually enough in well cut trousers with a cashmere sweater over an open-neck shirt, but no one would have mistaken him for anything but what he was. A man who commanded vast empty spaces that ordinary men would find daunting.

His eyes held hers as the lift doors opened in front of her. People filed out but she didn't move and a pathway seemed to open up as he walked towards her.

'Hanif…'

Lucy felt as if the air had been knocked from her body and he caught her shoulders as if afraid she might fall. He was always catching her before she fell, she thought.

'You called,' he said.

'I only just got the message that you rang back,' she managed. 'I was in Paris…'

'Paris?' He smiled. 'You are living life with a capital L…'

'No. It's my job… What are you doing here? Is Ameerah with you? When did you arrive?'

She was gabbling, talking too quickly, asking too many questions, but not the important one. The one that mattered.

Why are you here?

'You called and I came,' he said in response to her thought. 'I would have been here earlier but I had to present my credentials at the Court of St James's this morning.'

She frowned. 'But doesn't that mean…'

'That I've delivered my report to the UN, that my new post is in London. I'm here as my country's Ambassador.'

'Don't tell me,' she said. 'You miss the rain…'

'I miss you. And since you are here, this is where I must be too.'

He'd had his hair cut, she realised. It lay in thick, soft, dark layers, shining under the street light, and she reached without thinking for the leather tie that she'd used to hold back her own hair.

The one he'd used to tie it back for her. The one that she shouldn't be wearing. Like the amber silk blouse. The black linen trousers…

'And yet you put the Queen before me?' she demanded.

He smiled as if no words could have pleased him more.

'When Her Majesty finds ten minutes in a busy schedule, it's a brave man who is prepared to ask her to wait, to tell her that he has someone more important to see. Besides, now that's done, I can concentrate my whole mind on you.'

'Oh…' Then, 'Your *mind?*'

'My mind, my body, take whatever part of me you want.'

She swallowed. 'Is Ameerah with you?'

'In London, safe in the care of her nanny. She cannot wait to see you.'

'I've missed her so much.'

'Just Ameerah?'

No. Not just Ameerah.

'Can it be,' he said, glancing at the men standing slack-jawed behind her, then slipping into Arabic, 'Can it be that you have found the life you were looking for and have no time to spare for me?'

'No! I will always have time for you, Hanif. I owe you my life.' She smiled up at him. 'It's finally on a path forward, thanks to you. I've found my mother—at least she found me. I'm starting university next autumn—'

'I'm glad for you, Lucy,' he said softly and at that moment she realised that her path forward had begun not when she'd walked away from him, but at the very instant she had met him, when he had scared her witless with his knife, had saved her from a fiery death.

'Have you found somewhere to live yet?'

'What?'

'In London.'

'No. I haven't even begun to look—'

'The embassy is conveniently close to the School of Oriental and African Studies.'

She did not ask him how he knew. He could read her mind… If only she could read his.

'The rooms are large. Fully furnished. There is every comfort.'

Her breath caught in her throat. For a man of Hanif's traditions, beliefs, there would be only one reason he would ask her to move into his embassy.

'Have you come all this way simply to offer me accommodation, Your Highness?'

'You begin to read my mind, as I read yours, Lucy. There is, however, one small problem. You will have to share.'

'A room?'

His hands slid from her shoulder to her hands. He clasped them in his, drew them close to his chest, to his heart. 'Share my life, my world. You called and I have flown from New York with my heart in my hands, Lucy. My future. I have come to beg you for yours. To ask you to be my only wife, my one princess, to be the honoured mother to Ameerah. To the children that may come.'

She bent to kiss his hands and when she looked up at him her eyes were misted with tears.

'You are my life, Hanif. My one love. You are my prince and the husband of my heart. My life is yours.'

EPILOGUE

'ARE you sure about this?'

Lucy straightened, refusing to give into the backache that had kept her awake all night, had been plaguing her all morning. Nothing, not even the imminent arrival of her first baby, was going to deprive her of the magic moment when she received her degree.

'You can't make it through dinner without a dash to the bathroom,' Han said. 'You'll never be able to make it through the entire ceremony.'

'They've given me a seat on the aisle so that I can take comfort breaks. Honestly, I'll be fine, Han.' Her darling looked so anxious that she reached out, rubbed her hand reassuringly against his arm. 'Just tell me that this ridiculous hat is on straight and then go and sit down.'

'It's perfect. You're perfect.' Then, 'If it's too

much, just get up and walk out. Everyone will understand.'

'Han!'

He kissed her and then, because there was nothing else he could do, he joined her mother and all the other proud family members waiting to see their loved ones receive their degrees.

The wait seemed endless for him as name after name was called. For Lucy, he suspected, it felt like an eternity.

'Her Highness Princess Lucy al-Khatib…'

He let out a sigh of relief. Another few minutes and they could leave.

She made it up the steps, graceful as a galleon in full sail, crossed to the Chancellor, the daughter of another royal house, who kissed her cheek as she offered her congratulations.

Then, as Lucy reached for the certificate, he saw her face change.

He didn't wait for her to turn to him. He was out of his seat and running towards her before she found him amongst the crowd.

* * *

Two hours later, Lucy, exhausted, watched as he took this newest member of the al-Khatib family from the midwife.

'Well?' she asked.

There had been an unspoken pact between them; neither of them had wanted to know whether the child they were expecting was a boy or a girl, but there was a wobble in her voice now, an uncertainty, a fear that he would be disappointed if this baby was not the son he had so longed for.

'Do we have Jamal or Elyssa?'

He looked at her, took her hand and raised it to his lips, before laying their newborn against her breast.

'We have a baby, my love. A beautiful, healthy baby.'

MILLS & BOON® PUBLISH EIGHT LARGE PRINT TITLES A MONTH. THESE ARE THE EIGHT TITLES FOR JANUARY 2007

MISTRESS BOUGHT AND PAID FOR
Lynne Graham

THE SCORSOLINI MARRIAGE BARGAIN
Lucy Monroe

STAY THROUGH THE NIGHT
Anne Mather

BRIDE OF DESIRE
Sara Craven

MARRIED UNDER THE ITALIAN SUN
Lucy Gordon

THE REBEL PRINCE
Raye Morgan

ACCEPTING THE BOSS'S PROPOSAL
Natasha Oakley

THE SHEIKH'S GUARDED HEART
Liz Fielding

MILLS & BOON®

Live the emotion

1206 Rom

MILLS & BOON® PUBLISH EIGHT LARGE PRINT TITLES A MONTH. THESE ARE THE EIGHT TITLES FOR FEBRUARY 2007

❦

PURCHASED BY THE BILLIONAIRE
Helen Bianchin

MASTER OF PLEASURE
Penny Jordan

THE SULTAN'S VIRGIN BRIDE
Sarah Morgan

WANTED: MISTRESS AND MOTHER
Carol Marinelli

PROMISE OF A FAMILY
Jessica Steele

WANTED: OUTBACK WIFE
Ally Blake

BUSINESS ARRANGEMENT BRIDE
Jessica Hart

LONG-LOST FATHER
Melissa James

MILLS & BOON®

Live the emotion

0107 Rom LP